Ruby Tears

The Shades of Us Trilogy Book 2

ABBY FARNSWORTH

This is a work of fiction. Names, characters, places, and incidents are products of the author's imagination or are used fictitiously and are not to be construed as real. Any resemblance to actual events, locations, organizations, or persons, living or dead, is entirely coincidental.

World Castle Publishing, LLC
Pensacola, Florida
Copyright © Abby Farnsworth 2022
Hardback ISBN: 9798354658268
Paperback ISBN: 9781958336724
eBook ISBN: 9781958336731
First Edition World Castle Publishing, LLC, October 17, 2022
http://www.worldcastlepublishing.com
Cover: Karen Fuller
Editor: Maxine Bringenberg

Table of Contents

Acknowledgments

As always, thank you to Karen Fuller, Maxine Bringenberg, and World Castle Publishing! You guys are amazing! Thank you to Jason McCrady and M.J. Lemon. Your support is so helpful. And another thank you to all my friends, family, and readers for encouraging me. You all know who you are, and you're awesome! I couldn't do it without you.

To my readers, this is our 5th journey together – how thrilling! I hope you all enjoy *Ruby Tears* as much as you did my first four books. And thank you for all your reviews and ratings. They are so helpful! Make sure you're prepared for some tears with this one. Happy reading!

PS: To my "inspirations," thank you.

Dedication

In loving memory of Mildred Hedberg – I bet the '50s were great!

"She walks in beauty, like the night
Of cloudless climes and starry skies;
And all that's best of dark and bright
Meet in her aspect and her eyes
Thus mellowed to that tender light
Which heaven to gaudy day denies."

- "She Walks in Beauty" by Lord Byron

Chapter One

BROKEN

James looked at me, his emerald eyes sparkling. He tilted his head to the side. I placed my hand softly on the lower part of his face. This was a moment I'd imagined over and over again, a dream worthy of being wrapped in a ribbon. The idea that he was mine again made my mind full of flowers and gentle love songs. Beautiful, I thought. Moments later, I brought my lips to his. It was like powdered sugar had fallen upon my tongue.

I'd waited so long for this moment. When he was human, I'd been so afraid of hurting him. The idea of injuring his frail form had plagued me. Of course, he hadn't been weak. James had been nicely toned with muscles that many teenage boys would have been jealous of. But compared to my immortal strength, he'd been a butterfly. James's mortal form had been breakable, too much so for me to really show him all of my love.

Our lives had been so complicated. I had fallen for James when he was human and despised myself for it. Taking his mortality had seemed like a crime. But when Pansy, a deranged werewolf, had torn his body to the brink of death, I had been given no choice. I could have let him die, but that had seemed unthinkable. And so I had decided to change him, making him an immortal.

The choice had been difficult. Yet, in the end, I hadn't regretted it. Our love was too strong to abandon. This was my chance. I finally had just the right moment to fall into this ocean of bliss. The contentment was beautiful. This brilliant moment was enough to fill my heart with sweetness.

Our lips crushed each others. I poured myself into him, relishing in our love. We had forever. This was our chance at happiness. His hands softly held my waist. They were strong now, even more than mine.

Every particle of his body had turned to porcelain. Like me, he was a stone statue. We were nighttime beings illuminated by the soft candlelight. I never wanted to forget this moment. In a hundred years, I could look back on this.

He pulled away, a look of confusion leaking into his eyes. "Who are you?"

For a moment, I was sure I'd heard him incorrectly. "What?"

James shook his head, pushing me from his lap. I fell onto the daybed beside him, absolutely clueless about what to do. James's face was perplexed. He looked entirely lost.

"I don't know who you are," he replied.

I sat there completely silent. How was this possible? We loved each other. He was my everything. James held my heart. He was my boyfriend, my partner. We were completely and wholly infatuated with each other.

How did he not remember me? I hadn't lost any memories after I'd been changed. My human life, and the people who filled it, were still firmly planted in my mind. Nina and Anya, my sisters, hadn't lost their memories, either. This made no sense. He couldn't forget this love. We'd fought so hard for this. How could it be over?

I felt as if he'd torn my heart from my marble chest and crushed it within his firm hands. Panic consumed my body. Every inch of my stone-like hands seemed to shake. It was as if I was falling into a black hole. My soul was practically screaming for him to love me, but his eyes held no compassion. I was nothing to him.

I wanted to say something, but I couldn't. It was as if my lips were glued shut. There were so many things I wanted to tell him. Yet how could I possibly communicate my love in a few simple words?

I remembered the way James had held me, the way his lips had caressed mine, and how he'd told me he loved me. He'd professed his love as if it was as natural as the sun rising in the sky. But now, he couldn't even remember it.

"James, I love you," I whispered.

He stood from the couch, holding his hands in front of him. "What am I?"

Would he be furious? If he couldn't remember who I was, he certainly wouldn't know what had happened. He had no idea what he'd become. James didn't know he was an immortal. How would I explain what he'd transformed into?

He didn't even understand that vampires were real. All the time we had spent wishing for this moment was nothing. It was all gone. Because if he didn't remember anything, it was almost like it never even happened.

"The last thing I remember is...something about a beach and a girl. She was beautiful, with black hair and eyes a pretty shade of blue. It's all so blurry, though," James said.

I brought my hand up to cover my gasp. He remembered the night we'd had our first kiss. It wasn't clear enough for him to know it had been me, though. His memory was fractured. James had forgotten our love.

If that was really the last thing he remembered, then I was just a stranger to him. He was still my James, but I was just a girl. To him, I was a mysterious vampire with black hair and blue eyes. There wasn't any love in his brief memory of our time together. It was just a mess of fractured seconds.

"It's me," I whispered.

He looked at me with skepticism. "What happened to me? Why don't I remember you?"

Tears were streaming down my face. I had to

tell him. There was no choice. It was my responsibility to tell him that he was a — a vampire. He had become a child of the night.

My voice was small. "You're a vampire."

For a moment, he seemed to be in disbelief. Then his eyes grew wide as his fangs slipped from his mouth. They sliced his lip, causing a few drops of blood to fall onto his fingers as he reached up to touch them.

My stomach lurched as I witnessed it. I hadn't really been prepared to see this. No matter how much I'd wanted to be with him, seeing him as a vampire felt strange. I handed him one of the glasses of blood I'd prepared for when he woke. My long, lavender dress flowed freely around my hips. It clung to my chest before falling down to the floor. I'd worn it to be beautiful for him, but he didn't even seem to notice. My heart was writhing in my chest.

James took the glass from my hand with a look of disgust on his face. As he brought it to his nose, desire flooded his eyes. James lifted the glass to his mouth, gulping its contents down. His lips were ruby-red. A few drops of blood fell from his fangs. I couldn't tell if I was disgusted or entranced.

I didn't know what to do. Part of me wanted to run into his arms, while the more sensible side of my mind told me to wait. After all, he had no idea who I was. I wasn't his girlfriend anymore, only a stranger. The reality of the situation was enough to make me freeze.

"James?" I whispered in a questioning manner.

He looked down at me, hunger evident in his eyes. "I need more," he replied.

I nodded. At least I knew how to solve that problem. Gently I took his hand in my own. Though James looked at me strangely, he didn't pull away. I led him away from my room and out the back of the tiny house.

He looked up into the night sky, gazing at the stars. They were beautiful, but I didn't notice. My whole world had come crashing down. The man I loved had no idea who I was. Not long ago, James had begged me to let him have my heart. Now, he was clueless as to how much I loved him. The irony was overwhelming. We had switched places. How was I the one desperate for love? He'd become cold while I'd become a melted puddle of emotion.

He dropped my hand, seemingly uncomfortable

with the prolonged gesture. I felt my heart lurching in my chest. There didn't seem to be much I could do to stop the tears from dripping down my cheeks. My heart was shattered. When I looked at him, tears drizzled down my cheeks like raindrops falling from a mournful sky.

This was a terrible nightmare. He should have remembered me. Yet somehow, his change had gone wrong. I was left alone to suffer through this. I hadn't even considered such a possibility. It was foreign, something I'd never heard of before. No one I knew had lost their memory after the change. Most people turned out fine. Of course, it took some adjusting. But through my time as an immortal, I'd never heard of someone losing their memories.

Maybe he'd hit his head when Pansy had tried to kill him. She had tortured him and let him bleed slowly, all because she was jealous of my sister, Anya. It had been sadistic, twisted in a manner that would have made anyone feel sick. Even though Pansy was dead, I'd never hated any other werewolf as much as I despised her. It was an age-old rivalry that I had thought to be mostly extinct when my sisters had fallen in love with werewolf brothers, but I had been wrong. For some of us, it was still alive.

The horror of that experience had caused so many bad things, but I'd never suspected this. Perhaps he'd lost his memory before I changed him. That was the only explanation I could give myself. Pansy had taken James from me in more ways than I could comprehend.

No matter how it happened, it was heartbreaking. Loving someone who had previously loved you was so, so hard. I still felt every inch of the passion I'd felt when James was human, but he didn't care. There was no longer a look of love in his eyes when they met mine. I missed his soft, human nature. Everything about him had turned to stone.

"Where are we going?" James asked.

"To hunt," I replied.

Chapter Two

HELPLESS

I led James through the woods down to a small, secluded area we used for hunting. I usually preferred blood bags, but it was necessary for all vampires to learn to hunt. When resources weren't available, we had to have backups. There was a sweet waterfall flowing into a little pond. The sound of clean, fresh water tumbling down from the rocks was loud enough to fill the uncomfortable silence. We hadn't spoken for at least a half hour. Vibrantly colored grass sprung up around the small enclosure, allowing it to look like the entrance to a magical land. Of course, I didn't need any more supernatural elements in my life. I already had plenty to deal with. Vampires and werewolves were complicated to the extreme.

The world stood still as I searched for the scent of an animal. Moments later, I caught the odor of a deer. James had evidently smelled it too. I looked at him, assuming he'd ask me what to do. But without a single glance in my direction, he took off running. I followed him immediately.

We flew through the woods at a speed too fast for any human to comprehend. James looked entirely natural in his immortal form. He wasn't hesitant or scared. I was relieved that one thing seemed to be going all right. His memory loss was horrible. Even so, he didn't seem to be entirely miserable. James had accepted his new identity. Unlike me, he didn't seem to be bothered by the loss of his mortality. He had far more in common with Nina and Anya.

He halted in front of me, frozen in place. I stood behind him, waiting for his first move. James didn't even seem to notice my presence. If he was aware of my body behind him, he wasn't concerned with it. This new, uncaring behavior was so unlike him. I yearned for the love and attentiveness he'd shown during his time as a human. Before, he had never taken his eyes from me. Now, he didn't even care that my heart was breaking.

James jumped forward, pouncing on a helpless deer. I stood there watching him sink his fangs into its frail form. This was a new James. He was no longer my love, no longer the man I adored. He had ceased to be the loving boy who had desperately craved my heart. I had turned him into this primal monster. The only thing he wanted was blood, and it was all my fault.

He stood up, leaving the blood-drained deer on the ground. Blood was splattered on his shirt and all over his mouth. I turned my eyes away from him, unable to look at what I'd caused.

The fact that he was a vampire didn't bother me. No, that wasn't it. If he had woken as my James, with caring hands and loving lips, I would have been happy. But he'd become a totally different person. Just like me when I'd first been changed, he was relying on nothing but his base instincts. Nina and Anya had never lost their personalities. They'd seamlessly transitioned into immortals. I had hoped the same thing would happen to James. And if he hadn't lost his memory, James probably would have still been the loving man who held my heart. But he didn't seem to know who he was, no less how much

I loved him.

He gestured to the dead animal in front of him. "Are you going to eat?"

I winced. Seeing him with blood dripping from his mouth with crazed eyes was just too much. "No, I'm not hungry," I replied.

He shrugged before sprinting back toward the house. I followed him, hoping he wasn't going to do anything crazy before we made it back inside. He was a newly-changed vampire and, therefore, hard to control. James's impulses and lust for blood were so strong they clogged his mind. The fact that he didn't have his memory wasn't helping him think rationally either. I wanted to help him, but I hardly knew how. I'd never done this before.

When I arrived back at the house, James was rummaging around my room, looking for a fresh pair of clothes. I released a small sigh of relief. At least he'd retained enough humanity to realize he shouldn't be walking around in a blood-drenched shirt. We were making progress.

"Do you need help? I asked.

He nodded, "Please."

I smiled slightly before turning to open a

drawer in search of some of the new clothes I'd picked for him. After pulling out a pair of jeans and a lightweight T-shirt, I walked toward him. Before I had a chance to turn away, he ripped his shirt off. I wanted to avert my eyes, but I couldn't. I'd never seen him without a shirt before.

James's chest was nicely toned. Every part of his body was like stone. His abdomen gleamed like marble in the soft light. I was glad he didn't seem to notice my staring. Before he slipped his pants off, I turned away. I faced away from him, but heat still rose in my cheeks. Nina and Anya would have giggled at my anxiousness, but I really didn't know what to do.

He cleared his throat, evidently indicating that he was finished. I knew my face was red, but I turned around anyway. He tilted his head to the side as if unable to understand my embarrassment. It was too strange to meet his eyes.

"Who are you, again? How am I supposed to know you?" James asked.

There was a huge lump in my chest. I wanted to cry, but I couldn't. I didn't want him to see me like that. After all, I didn't want him to feel guilty.

"Your girlfriend," I whispered.

His eyes grew wide. "You're my girlfriend?"

I nodded. "Yes."

He walked over, so he was only a few inches away from me. "So, what happened to me? Why don't I remember being with you?"

I wanted to run into his arms, but it didn't feel right. He'd given no such invitation. James's body no longer invited me closer.

"We were in love, but then this werewolf girl kidnapped you and—well—it's a long story. If I hadn't changed you, you would have died. But the werewolf, Pansy, tortured you. I think somehow you must have hit your head and lost your memory," I replied.

I attempted to control the tears dripping from my eyes. It was hopeless, though. Just thinking about seeing his crumpled form on the floor of that dusty house was too much. It had broken me.

He took one of my black curls within his fingers and began twirling it around. I felt my breath catch. This was the first time James had initiated contact since he'd woken up. Perhaps something within his soul still loved me.

"You saved my life?" James asked.

I nodded. Tears were falling down my cheeks. He reached out to wipe them away, his snowy thumb brushing against my own pale face. I sighed, unable to prevent myself from crumbling against him. He caught me as I fell toward him, his arms hesitantly wrapping around my back.

Moments later, the door flew open, and Nina burst into the room. It was the first time I'd seen her since she'd retreated into her room with Roy after their wedding. She looked lovely. Her silky black hair fell gently to her shoulders. She wore a pretty green dress that ended at the top of her thighs, highlighting her brown legs. I'd always admired her beautiful form. She was confident in her body, and I was happy for her. I'd never met another woman from India, but I imagined that Nina would have been beautiful by almost any culture's standards. She was just…well, lovely.

A huge smile bloomed across her face, and she darted toward us. She embraced both of us in a hug, holding us close. James didn't seem to know what to do.

"Um, hello?" James questioned.

Nina was oblivious to his unaffectionate greeting. "How are you? Have you gone hunting?"

James looked at me questioningly. "Who is she?"

Nina's mouth fell wide open. Her eyes held fear as she stepped away from him. It was uncomfortably silent. I wanted to compose myself, but I didn't know how.

"He—he forgot everything. It's all gone. His memory of me, everything," I sobbed.

Nina wrapped me in her arms, gently calming me. "Oh, Anne, I'm so sorry."

I didn't respond. Her holding me was enough. She seemed to understand. Nina had always done this. When my vampire life had brought chaos, she had taken care of me. It was always what she did. Nina was just that kind of a maternal best friend.

"It'll be all right, love," she whispered. "He must have been hurt during the fight. His memory might come back. Maybe he's in shock."

I nodded. "I hope so."

She held me tighter. "Either way, his love will come back. It's deeper than memory, Anne. It's buried in your hearts. There's no way to get rid of true love."

We both seemed to remember that James was in the room and stepped away from each other to look at him. He was clearly perplexed. There was so much explaining to do. Where were we supposed to start? There wasn't a handout for this type of situation.

I motioned toward Nina. "James, this is one of my sisters, Nina."

He looked surprised. "You mean there are more people here?"

I nodded. "Nina's husband, Roy, my other sister, Anya, and her boyfriend, Arthur."

"Roy and Arthur are currently in the middle of their transformations," Nina added.

"Into vampires?" James asked.

I nodded. James didn't seem surprised or disturbed. He walked across the room and picked up another glass of blood. I'd never seen any other vampire so thirsty. He was starving. The fact that he was drinking blood didn't seem to bother him at all. James sipped on the cup as if it were a glass of wine. At least this was more refined than earlier when he'd slurped his first glass down. Of course, even that had been better than the ravenous way he'd attacked that deer. He acted like a rabid vampire, not the shadowy figures of myth.

It all made my stomach lurch. He licked the blood from his lips with a flick of his tongue. Nina didn't pay much attention, but she hadn't seen the way he'd attacked his previous food. I was just glad he was starting to act kind of human. Still, he wasn't well-adjusted.

"Well, I'll give you some privacy," Nina said.

I didn't want her to go. Honestly, I had no desire to be alone with him, not when he wasn't himself. It was so hard to look at him, knowing I had done this. If I hadn't fallen in love with him, he would never have been hurt. Because of me, he had to start life over. James had only wanted to become an immortal so we could spend forever together, but now he couldn't even remember who I was.

The idea of kissing him felt wrong. He wouldn't feel the same way about it as I did. I was no longer the woman he loved, just a pretty girl. He didn't know my heart. Well, there was a part somewhere within James that knew who I was, but I wondered if that tiny piece would ever resurface again. For now, I was a stranger. Strangers didn't kiss or hold each other, at least not in the way I desired. I needed intimacy, not just his body.

Nina walked to the door, closing it behind her. I stood still, not knowing what to do. I couldn't love him as I'd planned to. We wouldn't embrace the way I'd imagined. I was utterly lost as to how to react.

"So, what was it like?" James asked.

"What?" I replied.

James moved toward me. "Being in love with me."

The candles provided a soft glow within my room. I still had the curtains drawn, so even though it was light outside, it was dimly lit indoors. The room suddenly seemed very small as he stepped closer to me. The space between us was melting. James kept moving closer and closer until our faces were inches apart.

"Anne?" James asked.

"Yes?" I replied.

His eyes were focused on mine. Green emeralds gazing into a dark blue, star-filled sky. Mixing together, they created a swirl of bluish-green beauty. His fingers grazed my cheek.

"What was it like?" James asked.

I didn't know what to say. How did you tell someone just how much you loved them? Was there even a way to express such affection? Were there words in existence descriptive enough? I wanted to tell him all of it, to give him a slideshow of our relationship, or put it in a song.

His eyes were wide and expectant. I couldn't focus on him; his fingers on my skin were too distracting. Bubbling warmth rose within my abdomen. I wanted nothing more than him. No matter how hard I tried, I couldn't seem to remember that he wasn't my James. This was a different man, one who had no clue how much I loved him.

"It was lovely," I whispered. "I don't know how to tell you any of this. It's so hard for me to explain what we had."

I paused only to find him looking down at me as I averted my eyes. It was like he was boring into me with pure fire as I stood below him. His gentle fingers cupped the side of my face, giving me an invite to move closer.

"Loving you...it was like falling into bliss. You made me feel alive for the first time in seventy years. When I lost my human life, I thought I'd never be happy again. But with you, I started to feel joy." I spoke as if the words were flowing from my lips like a song.

"And this love," he whispered, "it was beautiful?"

"Very," I replied.

He leaned toward me, nuzzling his cheek against the top of my head. I placed my hands on his chest, feeling the cold surface beneath them. His fingers slowly found their way to my hips.

"I wish I could remember," he said.

I laid my head against his chest. "James...."

"Shh, Anne, it's all right," he answered.

James pulled away from me, and I frowned at the loss of his arms. I wanted him to hold me. But moments later, he pressed his lips gently to mine. It wasn't like many of our other kisses. There was no heat or quickness. Urgency wasn't present. It felt like exploration. He was trying to see who I was and how we were connected. Just feeling the silk-like taste of his lips against my own was enough to make me relax. I could almost forget everything.

He pulled a little away from me to murmur. "I wonder if we keep doing this, my memory will come back."

"Good idea," I replied.

Butterflies flew through my stomach as he wrapped his arms around my back and picked me up. I continued to place soft, gentle kisses against his lips. It was like we were afraid of hurting each other.

Our love still existed. It was just hidden. My heart was linked to his. We were meant to love each other. Some things weren't controllable.

"I see why I fell in love with you," James whispered.

Everything inside me grew tight as I tried to calm myself. I felt a tingling sensation travel through my arms. Love makes every inch of your skin erupt in sensation. His blond hair was tangled in my fingers as I pulled away.

"I'm glad," I replied.

Chapter Three
Why?

James was rifling through the books in the living room. I sat on the couch, watching as he attacked the bookshelf. A few of my favorites were scattered across the floor: *Jane Eyre, Emma,* and *Gone with the Wind.* They were books from my childhood, ones I would never forget. He was running his fingers along the pages of *Black Beauty.* James's movements were graceful and swift. He'd so easily adjusted to his immortality.

We hadn't spoken of our kiss, or rather kisses, since we'd exited my bedroom. Neither of us really knew what to do. I still loved him, and he was trying to figure out how he should feel about me. I wondered if perhaps anything would ever be the same.

Was this maybe worse than if he were dead?

Was it preferable for him to lose his memory rather than fall into peaceful death? Which was better? He seemed all right, but James had always been one to accept things easily. Some parts of his personality were the same. Though when I looked at him, I felt as if my heart was bleeding. I'd lost him, yet he was right in front of me. It was the strangest pain I'd ever felt.

Roy and Arthur had awoken hours ago. They were out hunting with Nina and Anya. Of course, they had woken perfectly intact. When Arthur had opened his eyes, the first thing he'd said was Anya's name. They'd kissed and cuddled until he could barely resist the need for blood. Roy had done the same. He'd woken up with a lazy grin on his face, his eyes glossed with desire to hold Nina in his arms.

It had made me so lonely. Arthur had given me a look of genuine pity when we'd told him about James. Roy's face had been covered in shock. Anya had held me against her tighter than ever before. They all realized how much pain I was in but couldn't actually comprehend its extent. This was the second man I'd lost.

My first love, Glen, had grown up with me

during World War 2. We had been childhood sweethearts. I had been sure of our eventual marriage. He had been everything a teenage girl could possibly want. My seventeen-year-old self had been infatuated. And when he'd been killed by the very same vampire who took my mortal existence, I'd wanted to be dead too.

After that awful night, I had spent seventy years alone. But when I found James, everything had changed. I'd fallen for him like a shooting star soaring through the sky. And he had loved me, too.

Now I was left mourning two men. Glen had been in the grave for decades, and James...well, his memory of me was lost. I wasn't sure which was harder to process. Both were so tragic, so dark that I wanted to curl into a ball and cry.

The door opened as Nina, Anya, Roy, and Arthur returned, their arms wrapped around each other. Seeing Arthur and Roy as vampires was still something I hadn't gotten used to. They walked toward me, sitting down on the couch. Roy sat beside me with Nina on his lap. They looked like matching stone sculptures from Ancient Greece: gorgeous and solidified. Arthur and Anya sat cuddled up on a loveseat near the empty fireplace. His arm was wrapped around her as she laid against his chest.

James, mostly oblivious to all of this, was still scanning the bookshelves. His every movement was as smooth as silk. There was no longer any human hesitancy or slip. It was all graceful. While I was lost in my thoughts of him, he turned around to face me.

His eyes drifted to the glass of chilled blood in Arthur's hand. Newly-changed vampires required so much blood. It was more than slightly overwhelming. They just didn't stop drinking.

"I'm confused," James said.

"About what?" I asked.

His voice was so beautiful. I craved every syllable, every word, and every line. Not one of his words went unnoticed. When he spoke to me, I was at full attention.

"Why don't we kill humans?" James asked.

Nina's mouth fell open, her eyes wide and perplexed. Anya was staring blankly at him. Her breathing had stopped. Roy had tensed, unsure of what to do. Arthur was frozen, still holding a glass of animal blood in his hand. I wasn't sure what to do. Why had he even asked that question? Wasn't it obvious? We respected mortality. Humans were valuable. We couldn't just go around killing them. That would have been monstrous. Every breath they took, every child that was born, was precious. Their heartbeats were like music.

"James, we respect humanity," I replied.

He tilted his head to the side in confusion. "Why? We're obviously better."

Nina's eyes were furious. "James, that's not true. Immortals are different from humans, not better."

He shrugged. "They'll die anyway."

"They deserve to live," Anya cut in.

"We were all human, once," Arthur added.

"But we're not anymore. What's wrong with enjoying immortality?" James asked.

"We're not telling you that you can't live a happy life," Anya replied.

Nina nodded. "We're just telling you that you can't kill people."

Arthur pulled Anya closer to him. She snuggled into his arms. Nina shifted uncomfortably. Roy was still in stunned silence. They all held expressions of fear. What would he say next?

James looked frustrated. "I don't understand. They're just like animals."

"They have souls," Nina interjected.

James pursed his strawberry lips. "Fragile ones."

No one knew what to say. He was acting like a vampire straight out of someone's nightmare. This wasn't how we behaved. We were civilized.

"I don't know if I agree with this. After all, they're just humans," James said.

I felt as if I might be sick. Every bone in my body seemed to shake. Nina put her hand on mine. It didn't help. James wasn't acting like himself at all, and it was all my fault. What if I hadn't changed him? At least he would have died with some dignity. He had been so caring, so loving toward me. James probably wouldn't have hurt a bug when he was human. Now he wanted to kill people, or at least thought it was justified.

"You don't have to agree," Nina replied. "You just have to refrain from your base desires. Eventually, you'll barely even think about it."

"I can't get it off my mind," he whispered.

I wanted to pull him into my arms. He needed

my love. It was so hard after the change. Every ounce of his body was yearning for blood. It would fade, but not right away. James's desire was overpowering. For a while, it would be his most fervent want. Just blood, always blood. And human blood, it was the best. I knew that. Killing humans was my biggest regret. It haunted me. Because no matter what I did, I could never bring them back.

I stood, walking toward him. "It'll be all right."

He took a step away from me. "No."

My heart lurched in my chest. Gravity seemed to pull me toward him, but I resisted. The look in his eyes held no warmth. This was what I'd feared. He didn't hate me, but he was indifferent toward me. Perhaps he was even angry because of the rules I was placing on him. His indifference might have been worse than the potential hate. At least fury was an emotion. It was tied to love. But this, it was blank. There was no passion, just a simple emptiness.

I loved him, though. Every single fiber of my body was attached to his. I wanted him. His love was what I craved. Even as a vampire, there was one thing I wanted more than blood. My desire to be loved was stronger than my urge to drink blood, even human blood.

I'd fed off James when he was still human, but only because of the closeness it had brought us. Of course, it tasted wonderful. But it made him happy, too. It wasn't all about the drinking. It was about us. When I fed, he felt good. That was what I loved most about it.

James didn't remember the way he'd held me as I drank from him. There was no memory of the bliss. Our love had faded into oblivion. I could still grab it, but it was gone from his sight. There was such a distance between us.

"I need to be alone," James said.

I wanted to reach for his hand. "I'll be here," I replied.

He didn't even bother to glance back at me before he darted away toward my room. I couldn't go back there, not with him. He didn't want me around.

I sunk to the floor, my back against the bookshelf. My pink dress flared out around me. My eyes met Nina's and then Anya's. They both held pity. I didn't want their sympathy, though. I wanted James.

There was nothing we could do. You can't

convince a bird to fly if they really don't want to. This was up to him. Roy and Arthur shifted uncomfortably in their seats. We were all lost. And even though I was crying, I couldn't shake the feeling that this was all my fault.

Chapter Four
WITH THE WIND

He was standing on the porch with his back toward the house. The rustling of my blue skirt had alerted him to my presence, but he didn't turn around. The light of the moon illuminated James's face, making him look like a dark, romantic prince. His blond hair seemed to glow, and his emerald eyes sparkled. James's deep red lips were pursed in a slight frown as he gazed out at the stars. He was beautiful.

Just looking at him hurt. I wanted to touch him, to hold him. But no, I couldn't. He hadn't kissed me again since that one blissful touch of our lips. Ever since then, he'd been physically and emotionally distant. I wished he would touch me, just the brush of a finger or touch of a hand. One tiny kiss would be enough.

"James," I whispered.

He turned toward me with a questioning expression on his face.

"You've been out here for hours. I just wanted to check on you," I said.

He shrugged. "I'm just thinking."

I handed him one of the glasses of blood I'd brought with me. It was in a glass cup that looked as if it had once been intended to hold lemonade or iced tea. It was crystal-like, with a delicate pattern on the outside of the glass. For a moment, I was back in my childhood. The sensation quickly faded as James's eyes met mine.

"Thank you," he responded.

He took a sip with a focused expression on his face. I followed his lead, taking a sip of my own drink. My tongue tingled as the liquid brushed my lips. It was all consuming. As the blood continued to slip into my mouth, it occupied my thoughts. There was no way I could focus on anything else. It was like being a heroin addict, or perhaps even something worse. This liquid ruled my life. I couldn't be independent from its sweet taste. It was like sugar on a pastry or hot chocolate on a cool winter night. Blood was what I lived on, literally. It was my sustenance, my source of energy.

James looked over at me, his lips wet and shiny. "What is this?"

"Lambs' blood," I replied.

He nodded. "I suppose it's better than the deer. Not as fresh, though."

What was I supposed to say? There was no question that human blood was the best. We all knew it. Even their scent was intoxicating. He hadn't tasted human blood, but it didn't take much to figure out the difference. Preferring human blood was as innate to vampire nature as knowing a steak was better than lettuce to a human. Survival was possible on the lesser foods but not enjoyable.

"I saw the bite marks on my neck," he said. "I know you used to bite me."

I closed my eyes. "It's complicated. We both wanted it. I didn't do it against your will."

He nodded. "So what, you just never expect me to try it?"

I bit my lip. "I don't want to deprive you of anything, but I can't agree to this. They deserve respect. We have to acknowledge their dignity and worth. Drinking from humans against their will is just as bad as rape. It violates them. Consent is the most important aspect. Without that, it's just wrong."

He shook his head. "You did it."

"It was consensual," I replied.

"And if I found a human who was willing, what would you say?" James asked.

My heart seemed to shudder. Did he see the intimacy of the act? Probably not. And if he did, he wouldn't care. I was just a girl to him.

"That would be up to you," I answered.

We stood in silence for a few more moments. He downed the rest of the blood. I couldn't drink any more — the thought made me sick. He wasn't acting completely crazy. The temptation was there for all of us, and I'd given into it before. The bite marks on his neck were an obvious sign of my drinking, of our love. It had all been voluntary. I'd never done it when he wasn't willing. He had asked me to do it. James had been so eager.

But to think of drinking from innocent humans who had given no permission or consent, that was wrong. I'd done it once, but there had been no one there to tell me it was wrong. I'd been lost and confused. James had me — he had all of us to tell him no. There was a difference. It didn't excuse what I'd done, the people I'd killed, but it was an explanation.

"We want to live different lives," James said in a small voice.

"I want mine to be with you," I whispered.

"I'm not sure if that's meant to be," he replied.

My heart sank. He really didn't want me, didn't want us. James had no memory of me and didn't seem to care about the love we'd lost. He had no intention of trying to rekindle it. That broke me, split every inch of my heart. Every fiber of my body felt fractured. He was tearing me apart. Yet if it made James happy to break me into nothing, perhaps it was all right. I wanted his happiness. Even if I faded away, his smile would be the same.

"I think I need to be alone for a while," he whispered.

I had known it was coming. But even so, it was more painful than I'd anticipated. I'd never felt rejection quite this hard. He was crushing my heart, but it was all right. If he wanted to be alone, that's what I would give him.

"James, just promise me you won't hurt anyone," I said softly.

Our eyes met, and for a second, he was my James. I felt a flutter in my chest. That same warm feeling rose from my abdomen and up into my lungs. My hand brushed his.

"I can't," he whispered.

I couldn't cry; I didn't have enough tears left. It was just sharp pain that flowed through every part of my body. I felt as if I couldn't get enough oxygen into my lungs. I imagined that maybe this was what a heart attack felt like. My body seemed out of my control.

"Don't go," I pleaded.

He looked at me with pity. "I'm sorry, but I can't love you when I don't know who you are. This isn't where I'm meant to be."

I couldn't say anything. It hurt too much. I just stood there staring at him. He looked back at me with an expression one might have had when looking at their sick grandmother. He was sorry but seemed to feel as if there was nothing he could do. James didn't love me. He only felt sorry for my pitiful state.

Gently he leaned forward and kissed my

cheek. His lips were soft yet hard. Gentle yet firm. They were the lips of a vampire. We were frozen. Two stone creatures awkwardly standing together, knowing it would be the end of whatever strange love had once been between them. That was really all we were.

"I love you," I whispered.

But when I opened my eyes, he was gone. It was over. The human I'd loved, he was a vampire lost to the wind. He was out there somewhere in the night. By morning, he could be virtually anywhere. I might never see him again. The thought made me want to crumble.

My love had left me, and he'd done it without hesitation. I was abandoned, stranded on the strings of former love. But it was all right because he might be happy. James was chasing contentment. It was a hard thing to find. I'd searched for it for years. Only when I'd been in his arms had I been at peace.

Nina opened the door and stepped onto the porch. She looked around for a moment. When she didn't see James, she turned toward me.

"Where is he?" Nina asked.

My blue eyes collided with her brown ones.

"Gone."

Chapter Five

Adorer

I started out watching the 1970 version of *Dracula*, but it was too depressing. Of course, not as depressed as me, but still. *Dracula* probably hadn't been the best thing to watch, considering that my ex-boyfriend was running around the South as a blood-hungry maniac. Then I'd moved on to the 1939 adaptation of *Wuthering Heights*. It was pretty good. I'd always liked it. When I was little, I would imagine myself as Cathy. The idea of running free among the English hills had been euphoric. As a little girl, there was hardly anything I could imagine as more romantic. I would have loved to own a horse, to ride upon the hilltops. My 1940s suburban childhood hadn't been the same as that of a London girl. But looking back, it had been just as magical.

I missed my Georgia home. Of course, I'd hardly lived anywhere else my whole life. We'd only come to Texas to escape Pansy in her mad rage. But now that James was gone, we didn't know what to do. Would we go back to Georgia? I didn't know what I wanted. It might be too overwhelming.

No one had talked to me. They didn't know what to say. Nina and Anya had knocked on my door several times, but I'd never answered them. I didn't want to talk. I just wanted to pretend as if I didn't exist. The TV and old movies drowned out my thoughts. As long as I didn't think of James, it would be all right. Of course, avoiding my memory of him was more complicated than I'd hoped.

Once the credits had rolled, I began watching *Gone With the Wind*. It was therapeutic. It wasn't my Georgia — not from my 1940s childhood or 1950s teenage years — but it was somewhat reflective of the place I'd come from. Sweet tea and sugar, cookies and cakes. I could taste the cherries and peaches, soft strawberries on my lips. The women with their swirling dresses, the men in dashing suits.

Just as Nina kept little statues, woven rugs, and sparkling jewels from India, and Anya kept leather satchels, clay vases, and earnings made from bone from her Cherokee heritage, I kept the memory of my Georgia. We had to hold tight to them. If we didn't, they would fade away. This was what we had. If I let it slip, I'd lose it forever. This memory was precious. To me, it was better than diamonds.

A plain white blanket was spread over my pink, cotton nightgown. I wouldn't sleep in it. That certainly wouldn't happen. After all, I was a creature of the night. But just the idea of sleep and its allusive beauty was enough to comfort me. My black curls fell down around my shoulders like a curtain made to conceal my porcelain skin. I heard Scarlett's voice on the TV and turned my attention back to her. We looked a little alike. The black hair, light skin, and blue eyes made us have a clear resemblance. She'd lost her love just like me. Maybe we were more similar than I'd once thought.

I could hear hushed voices in the other room. Everyone else seemed to be in the kitchen. The telltale sound of knives chopping lemons and limes on the counter gave away their location. Nina's voice traveled through the air as a soft giggle escaped her lips. I imagined that Roy was attacking her with kisses or wrapping his arms around her waist. Anya and Arthur were discussing something, though their voices were too low for me to hear. I wished that I was as happy as them. If only James hadn't forgotten everything, I would have been.

The smell of blood mixed with citrus enveloped my senses. Nina knew it was my favorite, but I liked cherries too. Though they were both my sisters, Nina had always been more of a maternal figure. She'd found me at my lowest and rescued me. Nina had taught me how to be a civilized vampire rather than a ravenous creature. Anya followed her lead, attempting to comfort me as much as possible.

Moments later, I heard a knock on my door. Before I had a chance to reply, it opened. I was expecting to see one of the girls, but when I looked up, I had a totally different surprise. Albert Jefferson, in his perfectly arranged suit, stood in front of me. He held two glasses in his hands. I didn't know what to say.

Albert had told me he loved me, but I'd turned him down for James. Everyone had thought I was crazy for rejecting a rich, Victorian bachelor for a teenage boy. Though I hadn't wanted to admit it, my heartstrings grew tight every time I saw Albert. The memory of his lips against mine was clear and precise. It was like watching a movie in my mind. I saw the way he'd held me, his strong hands against my waist.

"Hello, beautiful," he whispered.

My eyes grew wide as I examined his immortal face. Deep brown eyes, dark, messy curls, and a small grin. My heart gave a little thud. How did he do this to me? My soul was shuddering.

"Hey," I whispered.

He walked toward me as I made room for him to sit. Our bodies brushed against each other as he sat beside me. He gently lifted my knees, so they fell over his lap, and the blanket was draped over both of us. He'd never seen me like this before. I looked sick, though that was impossible for a vampire. Albert handed me one of the glasses he'd brought into the room.

"Nina and Anya called me," he said. "I wanted to come. I had to see you."

I took a tiny sip. "I'm sure you don't like what you see."

He smiled. "You're as beautiful as ever."

I lowered my eyes. The ache for James within my heart was still strong. "Thanks."

"I'm sorry," Albert whispered. "I know how much he meant to you. You gave him everything."

I nodded. "He left."

Albert pulled me against his chest. "I know, dove. I know."

I let myself fall into him, a few tears dripping onto his jacket. He didn't seem to mind. Albert wrapped his arms around me. Our glasses of blood had ended up on the table beside us, still mostly full. This was better than drinking. His scent and hard body gave more to me and my senses than blood could. He was overwhelming. How could one man distract me so much?

He smelled so fresh, so clean. Yet there was still a gentle touch of musk in his scent. We melted together into what felt like a puddle of stone. Two hard bodies wrapped in an embrace to create a jumbled mesh of marble. He seemed so relaxed as I lay on top of him. My face was buried against his body.

"It'll be all right, princess," he said.

"Why did you come?" I asked.

"Because I love you," he whispered.

It wasn't the first time he'd told me he loved me. Albert had fallen for me long ago. But then I'd met James, and my whole world had shifted. I'd never known a teenage boy could change my world as much as James had. He'd been a bright star in my otherwise desolate night. We had been beautiful.

"I'll take care of you," Albert mumbled with his cheek pressed against my head.

I thought of James, the way our lips had touched, and how lovingly he had looked at me with his soft, human eyes. He'd taken my heart. Every single cell of my body had been devoted to him. It had been real, true love. But now that he'd abandoned me, what would I do? Was it necessary to hold a devotion to him?

And Albert, I knew what he wanted. He'd never stopped pursuing me. Albert had given me space, but he'd still been waiting for my heart. I didn't know how I felt about him. At the moment, my heart was torn. James had lost his memory and didn't want me, but I couldn't simply transfer my affections. It didn't work like that. No matter how hard I tried, I couldn't rid myself of my thoughts of

James.

"I don't know what I can give right now, Albert," I whispered.

His hands grew tight around my waist. "Nothing, love. I don't expect you to give anything."

I relaxed into him as his lips pressed against the top of my head. It was as if my body, wrapped in my cotton nightgown, had somehow become molded to his. He didn't seem to mind but rather pulled the blanket up tightly around us. His hands floated gently across my hair and down my back.

I let out a soft sigh as I heard the TV continue to play and Rhett Butler say, "You should be kissed and often and by someone who knows how."

"But just so you know," Albert said, "in the morning, I'm taking you to London."

I didn't have the strength to argue.

Chapter Six

DORMIR

Nina and Anya had known all about the whole London conspiracy. Apparently, they'd talked Albert into the secret plan. Of course, he hadn't objected. When I walked out of my room in the morning wearing a pink sundress and heels, Albert had been smiling like a kid on Christmas. His grin had given me a little smile.

"You need to get out of the house," Nina had said.

"You need fresh air," Anya had told me.

"It'll be good for you," Arthur had added.

"Definitely," Roy had agreed.

And so, I'd been persuaded to board a private plane headed for London with Albert as my sole companion. I wasn't entirely sure why I'd chosen this path, but I was pretty sure it had something to do with peer pressure. It wasn't all that bad. Really, the plane was very nice. Leave it to Albert to have his own plane. He had everything.

There was a compartment up front with cushioned chairs, a large table, and a TV. On the wall was a mini refrigerator stocked with blood. Beside it was a bookshelf with glass doors that I hadn't wanted to open, afraid they'd fall out and tumble on top of me. I was tempted to touch one of them, just to feel their leather against my skin, but my fear of an avalanche of books was too terrifying. They looked so old and worn, like the kind of books you'd find at an antique shop. The pages would have been thin and fragile. Beautiful books, even if I could only look at them.

The middle of the plane had a couch, desk, and antique phone. The sofa was a deep purple in the cabriole style. It was plush with cushions that felt like feathers. Albert's desk was dark wood, with a large drawer and a hard-looking chair in front of it. The windows were covered by thin curtains that I pulled to the side. I liked seeing the sky. Flying was a sensation I rarely felt. I'd never liked crowded planes.

But this, the freedom it brought me, was wonderful. I felt like a bird.

The sky was at my fingertips. We flew through clouds like eagles soaring above the sky. It was magical. And down below us was the deep, enchanting sea. The water looked still from this far up. It was endless and expansive. I wondered how anyone had ever been brave enough to travel it.

In the back was a bedroom. I didn't enter it. Just glimpsing his room felt like an intrusion of space. But I didn't seem to be able to stop myself from looking at it. I thought I'd take a small glimpse for the sake of discovery. Albert was in the front of the plane with the captain, so he wouldn't see me. Besides, he'd left me alone. Was I really doing anything wrong? I was just taking a little look.

I pushed the door open slightly, not moving my feet. I didn't want to step into the room—that would have been too much. It would have felt wrong. Yet this whole action seemed to be an indication of something. I didn't want to think about what it was. Perhaps I could convince myself it was curiosity. That was partially true. I wanted to see more of Albert. Somehow his bedroom felt like a nice place to start.

The whole room was black. The large bed was covered in a velvet duvet the color of midnight. Fluffy pillows lined the headboard, and a black curtain surrounded the bed. Like the walls, everything on the bed was the color of a raven. Even the carpet was a luscious shade of black. It all appeared soft, too. Looking into the room was like staring into a dark abyss. It was illuminated only by a small chandelier.

It was all so private. I felt like an intruder in a secret space. It looked like a sanctuary for him, a place he could hide. Perhaps this was where he went when he wanted to be alone. Maybe he flew around the world for no reason other than to escape reality. He had so many people to impress, vampires to feed, and businesses to run. Yet when he was tired, he must have come to this room. I was staring into a space that was his own. In that brief moment, I saw a new part of Albert Jefferson.

I'd been so immersed in my contemplation that I hadn't heard him come up behind me, "Anne?"

In shock, I fell forward and tumbled into the room. I landed with the soft carpet beneath me. All of a sudden, I felt like a thief. I'd taken his privacy.

"I'm sorry," I whispered.

He looked confused, leaning over to help me up from the floor. "Don't be. I didn't mean to scare you."

"I shouldn't have been looking at your room," I replied.

He raised an eyebrow. "You're allowed to come in here. I wouldn't have brought you on the plane if I'd intended for you to stay out."

I bit my lip, careful to not let my fangs puncture it. He grabbed my hands and slowly pulled me up, so I stood against him. Albert's fingers traced the outline of my face. I shivered a little.

"Albert," I whispered.

He looked at me softly. "What, love?"

"I-I don't know. I don't know anything. Not how I feel, or what I'll do," I replied.

His finger traced my cheek and jawbone. His touch was frigid and sensitive. He was being as gentle as possible for a vampire. I wanted to lean into it. His touch made me lightheaded.

"That's all right," he whispered.

"I don't know what I can give you, promise you, right now," I mumbled.

"Anne," he replied.

I tilted my eyes toward his. They were dark and overpowering. Their hidden depths were slightly scary yet somehow comforting. They were hot chocolate or maybe a dark cup of coffee. Or at least that's what they looked like to me. Perhaps many would have seen darkness within his eyes. But I knew him too well for that. He was just Albert.

"I don't care what you can promise right now," he said. "I just want you to give me a chance."

James flashed before my eyes. His blond hair, soft skin, and grin were precious. But those were gone now — they had been for a while. James wasn't human anymore, he didn't remember me, and he'd walked away. That had to mean something. Did I have to forget him before I started thinking about Albert? It was possible to love them both.

"Okay, a chance," I replied.

He smiled. "Thank you."

Albert gently pulled me toward him, his lips pressing against mine while his hand tangled in my hair. My fingers were on his neck, rubbing softly against his cold skin. I felt lightheaded, almost dizzy.

He nuzzled his face against my cheek. I took a step backward, accidentally tripping and falling behind the curtain onto the bed. I'd never felt so clumsy in my life. He moved toward me, his eyes curious.

"I should get up," I mumbled quickly.

"You don't have to," he replied.

"Albert...," I whispered.

"You can just rest if you like," he said.

The velvet was soft beneath my skin. I wanted to lay down and close my eyes, maybe listen to some music. It was the closest thing to sleep I could get.

"Just rest?" I questioned.

He nodded.

I looked up at him. "How many girls?"

He looked confused. "What?"

"How many have you brought in here?" I asked.

"Just you," he replied. "Well, I let my sister borrow the plane once. I don't think that counts, though."

I grinned. "No, that doesn't count."

He nodded, smiling softly. "Rest, you need it."

He began to turn toward the door. I watched him pull the handle as he began to shut it. Albert suddenly wasn't the richest vampire in Savannah.

He wasn't an aristocrat or a billionaire. To me, he was only Albert.

"Don't go," I whispered.

He froze. "You want me to stay?"

I nodded. He turned around with hope in his eyes. I'd never seen so much joy. Slowly, he walked over and slipped his shoes off. He undid his tie and set it on the nightstand. Albert laid down beside me in his dress shirt, pants, and socks. I placed my hand on his chest, imagining what it had felt like when he had been human.

His face was hard, the way a man's might be when he was deep in thought. Albert generally had a way of controlling himself very well but now seemed to be an exception. His usual grin had been replaced with a look of contemplation. This was a side of Albert that I very rarely saw. It was only when we were alone in moments like this that he let his guard down. It was as if I'd peeled the shell off an egg. He was raw and open. Albert's messy hair fell against the sides of his face. His brown curls looked like spirals of silk. The white, colorless skin of his face was so vampire-like that it almost made me want to laugh. He was gorgeous, like a statue that was stuck in a permanent pose of deep thought.

"I hope you won't get bored, just laying here while I think," I whispered.

"Don't worry," he said. "This is the only place I want to be."

Chapter Seven

Paramour

After a while, I got restless, lying quietly within the velvet covers recounting the events of the past month. I'd met a human boy, James, and fallen in love with him. He'd found out what I was and accepted it. I'd started feeding on him, but only when he asked me to. We loved it. Bites gave both of us so much pleasure. Relaxation for him, elation for me. James had grown so comfortable with what I was that he'd asked me to turn him. With much persuasion, I agreed. I didn't want to spend eternity without him. But before I had the chance, a crazy werewolf girl out for revenge against my sister had kidnapped him. He'd been close to death, but I'd saved him. Then when he woke, he hadn't remembered who I was. James had chosen to leave me. The idea of an animal diet hadn't satisfied him. And so, here I was.

Albert was still beside me, lying peacefully while I thought. He'd been through this with me. In the middle of this disaster, he'd told me that he'd been in love with me for years. I'd rejected him because of James, only later realizing that I held feelings for him. Albert held no grudge against me for saying no. He'd come to my rescue, sweeping me away from Texas and onto a plane on its way to London. We were going back to his hometown.

I could feel his hand rubbing against my fingers as he lay beside me. Each time my skin touched his, it was overwhelming. He wasn't the same as James, not soft or warm. He was a vampire. Albert and I were two creatures of stone, romanticized in pop culture and thought to be fictional by many. We were creatures of myth, but for us, this nightmare was real.

Yet as I felt the nearness of his body, I didn't mind its lack of humanity. His eyes held all the softness a human could possess in their entire body. His hands carefully evaded most of my form. He never ventured from my fingers, hands, and arms. Never once had he tried to kiss me while I thought.

My contemplation had been uninterrupted.

I reach up to stroke his face. He leaned into my hand, exhaling as he felt my skin against his. His cheek was as hard as a rock and smooth as silver. His body was as gorgeous as marble. For the first time since we'd started this journey, I felt the need to be closer to him. So, so much closer. I wanted him to hold me.

"Albert," I whispered.

His dark eyes were sparkling like jewels in a hidden cave. "Yes?"

I bit my lip. "I want...."

He reached up to touch my cheek. "Anything."

Slowly, I moved toward him. He held his arms open for me to melt into him. It felt good, just being wrapped so tightly that I didn't have to worry about anything else. I needed release, relaxation. Albert could give me everything, and I wanted him to. I never wanted him to hold anyone else. His arms were mine.

His cheek touched my hair as he nuzzled against me. Albert had no idea what I wanted. Well, at least not all of it. I had to show him. He wouldn't believe me, not at first.

I slipped my hair off my shoulder and moved even slower toward him. Placing a soft kiss on his lips, I wrapped my arms around his neck. He sighed, so obviously at peace.

A moment later, I pulled his head down toward my neck. "Please...."

He looked at me in shock. "No, you hate it. I know how you feel about being bitten."

"Albert," I mumbled. "Please, I want this. I want you."

His breathing quickened. "Anne, I don't want to lose you. I can't have you run away."

I understood why he was scared. He'd bitten me once, before James, when he'd asked me for a dance. We'd gotten somewhat carried away. But after he bit me, I ran away. At that point, I hadn't processed the trauma of my first bite, the time when I was changed. After my failed relationship with James, I came to understand that a bite didn't always mean violence. It could express so much, even love. It brought pleasure and satisfaction. And true, biting a vampire wasn't the same as with a human. But still, it would show Albert how I felt about him. There weren't words I could say, but I could give him this.

"If you don't do it, I will," I replied.

He seemed to notice the intensity in my eyes, and moments later, he acted on it. With vampire speed, he pulled me against him and sunk his fangs into my neck. This time it didn't bring fear or anger, only bliss. I sighed as I felt the endorphins flooding my mind. It was Albert. I was safe.

I could barely even feel what he was doing, but the gentle suck was like a pulsing sensation in my neck. It hardly compared to the feeling of his hands on my back and arms around my waist. I touched his hair, wrapping strands of it within my fingers. I didn't know what to say. Was it love I felt?

Before I'd even become completely immersed in the sensation, the door to the bedroom flew open. I screamed, and Albert pulled my head down to be tucked against his chest. The feeling of floating still consumed me. He seemed to have more of his senses.

I recognized the voice of the pilot. "Sir, I'm so sorry. I wanted to inform you that we've landed."

I felt Albert's body stiffen. "It's all right. Thank you. Next time, please knock."

The awkwardness radiated through the room as the captain spoke. "Yes, sir."

The door closed as Albert pulled me up so I could look into his eyes. I was a little dizzy, but all right. If I were a human, his face would have scared me. His fangs were still present, and his chin was covered in blood. It had splattered over both of us, spilling onto my dress and his shirt.

"Sorry, love, we have to go," he whispered.

I nodded, a little disappointed. But before he rose to change his shirt, I replied. "Albert, I'm pretty sure I'm in love with you."

He looked at me with absolute tenderness. "I know, baby, I know. And trust me, I love you too."

~*~

After he changed, Albert handed me a bag with more clothes than I could have possibly needed for such a short flight. He apologized for the small selection and assured me he'd ordered more to have ready at his townhouse. Of course, I'd been entirely overwhelmed. But it wasn't the craziest thing Albert had ever told me. At this point, I was getting used to it.

After searching through the bag, I pulled out a blue dress with ruffles that fell down to my mid-thigh. It was about the same color as my eyes. I wanted to wear something he would like. Things like that seemed important now.

There were shoes too, of course. Without much thought, I picked a pair of black, block heels. I organized my curls, arranging them in the most sensible form possible. But still, they looked unruly. Albert seemed to like that, though. Tonight, I was like a sixteen-year-old girl. I was a fanatic about a boy, and it felt wonderful. I felt alive for the first time since James had died and come back. I didn't have to worry about a human boyfriend or if I was drinking too much from him. Right now, I could let myself be taken care of.

Albert watched me as I slipped a pair of diamond earrings on. They had been a gift from Nina. When you had forever to live, there were few things you could give each other. Nothing seemed right. But one Christmas morning, I had found these placed under the huge tree that Anya had dragged into our apartment. I only wore them when I was feeling beautiful, and tonight was one of those times.

"Who are they from?" Albert asked.

I grinned a little. "You really shouldn't be jealous of my sister."

He rolled his eyes. "Well, I had to make sure."

I laughed. "You're adorable."

He walked over toward me, placing his hands on my hips. "You didn't seem to think that earlier."

I shivered. "Well, maybe I'll change my mind again."

He laughed. "Maybe."

There was a knock on the door. "Sir, your sister called again. She's expecting you."

He groaned. "We're coming."

Albert grabbed my hand and pulled me toward the door. I followed him. Tonight, I didn't want to fight. I hadn't relaxed in so long. But with Albert, it felt possible. I could be a girl. That was what I wanted to be. Just a girl in love. He let me feel beautiful. With him, I imagined a world free from anxiety. I could just exist. That was an incredible thing. With our arms wrapped around each other, the world seemed calm. Everything faded away.

A car was waiting for us when we left the airplane. I leaned into Albert as he held me against him in the car. It was late, and I liked it. The moon shone above us as I saw London for the first time. It felt right seeing it in the dark. After all, this was supposed to be my habitat. Embracing it wasn't a bad thing. Besides, it felt romantic. The city of rain and fog was bringing me within its grasp. So much mystery was packed within this place. A town where anything could happen.

Albert handed me a drink. "I took a lot from you. I'll feel better if you replace it."

The blood was sweet against my lips. "Aren't you going to have one?"

He laughed. "Trust me, sweetheart. I've had plenty."

The stars were shining above us as I stepped out of the car and onto the sidewalk, Albert right behind me. I looked up at the impressive structure he called a townhouse.

"I thought it was supposed to be small," I said.

He shrugged. "It kind of is. I mean, the house is smaller than some. It's a bit relative."

It was beautiful. The house was a tall brick structure with a Parthenon-style entrance that made it look ancient. Vines, well kept and pretty, traveled up the structure. The windows were clean and elegant, with white curtains flowing in the wind. There was a balcony on the second floor that looked as if it belonged in a fairytale castle. The house was three stories tall and larger than most of the surrounding structures. Flowers bloomed in the small yard — roses, white and red, beautiful enough to make me want to pluck them from their bushes.

"You like it?" Albert asked.

"Very much," I replied.

He smiled. "We can stay as long as you like."

"That might be a little while," I whispered.

He chuckled before taking my hand and pulling me toward the door. I stepped through the little garden up onto the doorstep. He smiled at me as he stroked my hair. Albert sighed. "I'd like to apologize in advance for this."

"For what?" I replied.

Before he had a chance to reply, the door opened. A small, older woman, a vampire, was standing behind it. She smiled endearingly at me. Moments later, she moved to reveal a tall, thin woman with dark red hair and a pair of pursed lips. Her eyes were tight, and her smile strained. The woman's long hair flowed down to her waist as silky as a curtain. Her outfit was a long corset dress. Its red fabric fell to the ground into a pool around her. It was about the same color as her hair but a little more maroon. She looked like a queen, the ruler of an empire.

Her red lips parted as she smiled. "Albert, I see you brought the American girl."

Albert rolled his eyes as we stepped into the house. "Her name is Anne, Hazel."

"I see," Hazel replied.

"Is there a reason you insisted on greeting me in the middle of the night? I was rather looking forward to showing Anne around," Albert said.

Hazel laughed. "Oh, my mistake, I'll leave you to your muse. I'll be back tomorrow, baby brother."

Albert gave her a stiff smile. "Can't wait."

She strode past me, her hair flowing behind her. With her dark red hair and matching dress, she looked a bit like fire. Real, true flames. They could have erupted from within her, and I wouldn't have been surprised, other than the fact that she seemed colder than ice.

Albert paid little attention to his sister as she walked out the door, the old woman closing it after her dress had vanished from the doorstep. He turned toward the woman, who I presumed to be a housekeeper of sorts, and smiled.

"Thank you, Juli," he said.

"Of course, Mr. Jefferson," she replied.

The woman gave me an encouraging smile as Albert pulled me toward the steps. I smiled back, noticing the glimmer in her eyes.

"It was nice to meet you, Ms. Emerson," she said.

"Thank you," I said before we reached the second level.

I glanced around at the second floor of Albert's house. It was too beautiful to accurately describe. Everything seemed to be in soft shades of grey with hints of red and bits of blue. A large British flag, which looked to be an antique, hung on the back wall. The doors that opened onto the balcony were clear and crystal-like. Dark wood extended along the floor. A large, soft-looking carpet lay in the center of the room, where a few velvet couches sat. The wall closest to me held a bookshelf that was probably twice my height and extended the whole length of the room. It was stuffed with piles upon piles of texts. Some of them were books, others letters or documents. Artifacts also lay upon the shelves. A few pieces of jewelry were enclosed within locked cases.

On the opposite side of the room was a blood bar that looked full enough to feed a room of vampires. On either side was a desk, each with its own set of pen and ink. Papers were scattered upon them. Some were old, others new. The whole room screamed his name. It was all so Albert.

I could have lost myself in that room. There were so many things to explore. Many of the books had to be originals. Some of the jewelry was probably ancient. To just exist around such things made me feel young. As I looked up, I saw that painted upon the ceiling in black and white was a map of the world. London, Savannah, and a few other cities I assumed he had a connection to were labeled. The whole room was like a sophisticated vampire man cave. It was a rather odd concept.

The only light illuminating the space was from a few lamps that gave off a dim, barely visible glow. It was dark and comforting. The room was cozy. Upon the walls were several portraits of kings and queens of old. Royalty and power emulated through the room. Sitting on one of the desks was an old photo of a man with dark curly hair, a fair complexion, and deep, mysterious eyes. It was Albert.

"This room is so you," I whispered.

He smiled. "Well, that's the point." He paused for a moment. "I wanted you to see me, Anne. To really see me. You've witnessed the mad, crazed bachelor who runs through Savannah without a care in the world. And that's fine because that life is a part of who I am. It was who I was when I was younger. I revert to it more often than I'd like to admit. But with you, I want to be better. You're so good, Anne. And when I look at you, I want to give you the world."

I walked toward him, placing my hands on his cheeks. "I want to see every part of your soul."

"You will," he whispered.

I placed a gentle kiss on his lips. It was soft like a butterfly landing upon a flower. He wrapped his arms around me and held me against him. His fingers tangled in my hair, allowing me to rest against his chest.

"I love you, little dove," he whispered.

"I love you, too," I mumbled back.

We walked up to the third floor, where a long hallway was located. Albert took my hand and began pulling me down along the corridor. The hallway was illuminated by sconces that looked as if they belonged in a castle. It was fitting. This was Albert's home. He belonged in London the same way I belonged in Savannah. Not only that, but he was vampire royalty. Not literally — such things didn't exist. But in reality, he was a prince. One of magic and beauty. He owned more property than was fathomable. He'd built this world for himself through hard work and determination. And now he was royal, not in title, but rather through practicality.

"This way," he said as he pulled me into one of the rooms. I stepped through the heavy door into a bedroom fit for a king. Long windows upon the walls were covered by black curtains. A tall bed that looked as if it had been stolen from a history documentary was in the center of the room, decorated in thick, royal blue covers that looked like real silk. Pillows upon pillows were stacked on top of the bed as if to create a castle of comfort. Laying upon it looked as if it would have felt like drifting atop waves.

Two nightstands sat on the sides of the bed. Candlesticks flickering with small flames rested upon them. They lit the room with the gentle light of history. Large, sturdy bookshelves were placed beside the nightstands. Unlike the ones on the second floor, these held no novels. There were several shelves dedicated to the American Civil War, others to the American revolution, and a few to British history. Piles of books were dedicated to European monarchy, others to Native American tribes, and some to the Antebellum South. He studied everything. There was a floor-length mirror on the wall opposite his bed. It was large enough to take up half of the wall. On one side of it was a wardrobe, a dresser on the other.

"What do you think?" Albert asked.

"I'm starting to think you're a historian," I replied.

He nodded. "It fascinates me. And I am very, emphasis on very, distantly related to the House of Tudor. I've traced it back myself. Through some ridiculously complicated digging and a few trips to confirm my research, I managed to discover my family history. It's too distant to be of any real importance, but it's interesting."

I raised my eyebrows. "That's incredible."

He smiled. "I thought so, too." He paused for a moment. "Not to sound like a stalker, but I traced yours as well."

An expression of shock crossed my face. "What?"

He shrugged. "I was curious."

Suddenly, my own curiosity seemed to spike. I'd always wondered about it. I knew nothing about my family's history other than that we'd been in Georgia for longer than anyone could remember. We were probably from Britain, though I didn't know for sure.

"Well, what did you find out?" I asked.

He smiled. "I was a little surprised. There was the usual Georgian ancestry. The typical southern aristocracy. If you go back far enough, it gets more fascinating. Most of your family came from Britain. But a small branch was from France. The House of Bourbon, to be specific."

My jaw dropped. "I'm a descendant of the Bourbon Dynasty?"

He nodded. "Impressive, isn't it?"

I began to smile. "Unbelievable."

He placed his hands on my waist. "Well, princess, now that you know the truth, let me show you to your room."

"I have a room?" I asked.

He shrugged. "Your sisters helped me with it."

I laughed. "Of course they did."

He held my hand as he led me down the hallway to another room. The heavy, plain white door opened to reveal one of the most delicate rooms I'd ever seen. The floor was a white carpet that looked like fluffy clouds. Several huge windows were open to reveal the moon and allow the night air to float into the room. In the center of the room was a huge, four-poster bed covered in a purple duvet. The pillows had an intricate golden pattern on them that matched the wallpaper. There were two purple divans the same color as the bed. Fairy lights were strung across the ceiling to create a magical look.

"It's so pretty," I whispered.

He smiled. "Wait until you open the closet."

I dashed toward the double door that opened to reveal a walk-in closet fit for a queen. A giant chandelier hung in the center of the room, illuminating the rows upon rows of dresses, skirts, and blouses. There were shelves stacked with pants, shirts, and jackets. And on the far wall was an almost endless array of shoes.

"Oh...," I whispered.

"Not bad, I hope?" Albert asked.

A huge grin spread across my face. "It's lovely. But Albert, why?"

He placed a small kiss on my forehead. "I love you, and that's not going to change. I want to be with you, Anne. Forever."

Standing in the middle of my closet in Albert's townhouse, I knew he was right. This was meant to be. I didn't know anything about fate, but I knew this was right. Loving two people wasn't impossible. James was still in my heart. I'd fallen so hard for him. But maybe he wasn't supposed to be my forever. Not everything gorgeous lasted for eternity. I had loved James passionately. But looking at Albert, I knew he was the one for me.

"I want to be with you, too," I replied.

"This is it, Anne," he whispered. "You need to know that if you say yes to me right now, I will refuse to let you go ever again. If you say yes, this is forever."

His dark eyes bored into mine. I traced the outline of his curls, the curve of his jaw, and the shape of his nose. Every part of him was a beautiful marble sculpture. He was a marvelous piece of art.

And I wanted him. Not just for a little while, but for the rest of my life. There was something between us. It had always been there. I'd denied it over and over again. When I'd loved James, I had buried it beneath me. But I couldn't anymore, not when I loved him like this.

It seemed so fast, but it wasn't. Because though I'd just separated from James, I'd loved Albert at the same time. My decision to be with him wasn't as sporadic as it seemed. This love had been boiling within me. Only now was it overflowing to the point where I couldn't deny myself the one thing I wanted. Albert was better than any imaginary man I could have made up.

Maybe this was why destiny had chosen me to become a vampire. If Albert and I had remained humans, we would have never met each other. In this strange world, it was the only way for us to be together. We had been born worlds apart. In some way, we still lived in different eras and times. But when his fingers brushed mine, I didn't regret being a vampire. I no longer resented it because it had brought me to him.

"Yes, Albert. Yes," I replied.

He exhaled. For a few moments, we stood still. I was slightly worried he'd gone into shock. I was about to ask if he was all right when he moved toward me and pulled me against him. Our lips crashed into each other. I couldn't stop. My love for him was like gravity. It was permanent. There was no way to get rid of it. It just pulled me closer and closer to him. Now that I'd given into it, I couldn't stop.

He wrapped his arms around my back before lifting me up so that my hands were in his hair. He kissed my neck over and over again. I nuzzled my cheek against his hair as he pressed soft kisses against my collarbone. A few moments later, his fangs sunk into my neck.

Chapter Eight

AMOUREUSE

Watching him work was an activity all by itself. I sat on the couch in his weird, vampire man cave, sipping a glass of blood. He sat at his desk, the one I had discovered was intended for business, while he wrote what seemed to be a long email. The person on the other end had either done something very good or very bad because Albert generally didn't stretch things out. He liked to be brief and concise. Well, when it came to everything except romance.

He didn't wear dress clothes today. It was an odd thing to see him in jeans and a sweatshirt. He never wore that type of clothing. But now, his dark hair was a mess of curls falling to the side of his face while his brows were scrunched in concentration. His posture was perfect, though. It was a vampire thing.

I was still wearing the little nightgown I'd changed into earlier. It was black with lace around the edges. Honestly, I kind of liked it. I would have never picked it out for myself, but it had been in my closet when I'd arrived. Albert did things like that. He'd probably never stop treating me like a prize he'd won. That was all right. I didn't mind. It made him smile, and that was enough.

He sat back in his chair, turning around to see me. Albert had a grin on his face that told me he had a plan. Of course, like a little girl, I was fascinated to discover what it was. Albert's ideas were generally extravagant. At least it would be entertaining.

"What's that look in your eyes?" I asked.

He smirked. "We're going out tonight."

I smiled back. "Where?"

"It's a surprise," he teased.

I rolled my eyes playfully. "Fine."

He laughed. "Go look in your room."

I raised my eyebrows in confusion before standing up and hurrying to my bedroom. I knew he was enjoying surprising me. As I walked up the stairs and down the hallway to my room, his footsteps were behind me. Maybe I could persuade him to stop working for a while. That would be nice. When had I become a giddy teenage girl?

I opened the door to my princess-like room to discover a long, silk gown upon my bed. It was a dark green color that was designed to frame my body until it reached my knees, where it would flare out in a river of smooth material across the floor. I reached out to touch the dress. It hadn't been in the closet before; this was new. Beside it lay a jacket made of black fur and a pair of silver, lace-up heels.

Albert's hands landed on my waist as he placed a gentle kiss on my neck. I smiled, reaching up to touch his messy curls. He sighed softly as he leaned in toward me.

"It's beautiful," I said.

He smiled. "I thought it would look nice on you."

I turned around and grinned. "Where are we going?"

"I'm not telling you," he replied.

I bit my lip. "Why not?"

He smirked. "Because it's so much fun watching you try to figure it out."

Albert had gone back to his room to get ready. We'd spent most of the day at the townhouse. He'd shown me his books of research on both of our families' histories. I was fascinated to see exactly who I was. From my Georgian roots to my Bourbon past, it all made sense. My bright blue eyes were so French. My pale skin and rosy lips certainly added to the look. My black hair was far more Anglo-Saxon, but Albert had found that in my genealogy too.

I imagined what he was doing in his room. Probably putting on one of his suits. Maybe black to match my jacket, with a green tie to go with my dress. His dark eyes would gleam in the candlelight of his bedroom. And when he came to find me, he'd be gorgeous.

I'd tried to look my best. The dress certainly helped with that. It was sleeveless, showing off my shoulders and collarbone. I'd never paid so much attention to my neck before. I still wore the diamond earrings Nina had given me. They looked wonderful with the silver heels. The dress was tight, but not so much that it hurt. It certainly didn't feel like a corset. My chest was propped up, allowing my abdomen to look even thinner than usual. I'd worn a thick, red lipstick that was almost too dark. The color was blood-like, more so than I'd expected.

Staring at myself in the mirror, I realized something. With my black curls, pale skin, red lips, and slender form, I honestly looked like a vampire. I'd never appeared so vampire-like as I did in this satin dress that made me feel like a model. But right now, I didn't mind. Usually, I preferred to look human. It made me feel more normal. And with James, I'd tried to pretend.

With Albert, I could be a vampire. He and I were the same. It wasn't strange that I survived on blood or never slept. My habits weren't inconvenient or odd. When I kissed him, I didn't have to worry. He was even more vampire than I. Albert had been living this way for over a hundred years. To him, this was life. I wasn't a freak show or something out of the ordinary. To him, I was just Anne.

It didn't have to make sense to me. I was okay with the fact that this had spiraled into something out of my control. I was in love with him, and I knew that. Maybe I had been for most of the time I'd known him. Who knew how long I'd felt something for him? There was something intrinsic about us.

It was natural, even easy. And he loved me. Albert truly adored me, and I enjoyed it. I wanted to be loved. And with him, I didn't have to hide.

I heard the door open and turned around to greet him. My jacket was still laying on the bed, and I wore nothing more than the gorgeous dress that made me feel beautiful. He approached me with a look of awe on his face.

"You are incredible," he whispered.

He was only inches away from me, and I reached up to kiss his cheek. "So are you."

He was dressed as I'd predicted. I was starting to understand him. He wasn't as much of a puzzle as he pretended to be. When he was with me, he showed his true self. We understood each other like that. Our souls were linked. We were connected in a way I didn't understand. Our energy matched.

He leaned down to reveal a silver choker with a single ruby hanging from it and clipped it around my neck. I didn't know what to say. Reaching up, I felt the ruby against my neck. It was about the same color as my lips.

"I wanted you to have it," he whispered.

"Where did you get it?" I asked.

He smiled. "It was my mother's."

My mouth fell open. "Shouldn't this belong to your sister?"

He shook his head. "She didn't like it. Hazel said it wasn't really her style."

"I'm not sure I should take it," I replied.

He took my face in his hands. "Anne, we went over this. You said yes to me. You said yes to our forever. It's all yours. Anything I have belongs just as much to you as it does to me. And one day, I'll prove that."

My breathing was heavy. I didn't know what to do. He was so much more than I'd ever imagined. This was a man who loved his family, who deserved to have one of his own. But we never could. It was impossible. Yet he so, so deserved this love. I would give him everything.

"You are more than I ever thought I'd have," I whispered.

He placed a light kiss on my lips. "I'm still not as much as you deserve."

~*~

London was alive at night. A fog had descended over the city, but it was still beautiful. In fact, the mist made it almost ethereal. We drove through an area with shops, bars, and restaurants that were so full of people I wondered if they ever slept. Men and women bustled around dressed for parties. The nightlife was brilliant.

Eventually, we reached an area that was far less populated. It wasn't run down, though. The street was calm. Pretty townhouses with flower-filled yards and pretty lanterns lined the road. Soft light floated out a few of the windows as the curtains blew in the breeze. It was a lovely setting. The night was mysterious and grand, beautiful and calm. I wanted to stay here. It deserved to be painted and written about. I was starting to love London. It wasn't Savannah, but it was something almost as wonderful.

We stopped in front of a tall, gothic building where a valet took the car. The building was lit by dim candles. Albert opened the tall, elegant wooden doors, and we stepped into a carpeted entry room. Within were lanterns that illuminated the small foyer. Albert took my jacket and hung it on one of the many hangers.

I felt as if I'd stepped into a medieval

masterpiece. The wooden floor was covered in a dark red carpet. The walls were shadowy with few windows and decorated with portraits. The paintings were old. The newest ones seemed to be Victorian, and the older ones had to be from before the Renaissance. Each inch of the room seemed as if it held a million memories.

Albert took my hand and led me down the hallway. As we continued, I began to hear voices. They weren't human but rather vampire. The syllables were slick and smooth. I'd never heard so many vampires together before. The house was devoid of human blood. I could relax.

He stopped in front of a carved wooden door and pulled it open. As soon as I walked in, I was amazed. Candles were everywhere, and satin-covered tables with flowers upon them filled the room. Vampires of all ages and backgrounds were scattered about. Some danced while others sat and talked. The windows were shrouded by dark black curtains. It was like a vampire banquet. Mystery and passion were everywhere. As I glanced around, I saw the flash of fangs and sparkling of immortal eyes.

"Let me guess, you own this too?" I asked.

He smiled. "You're getting good at this."

"So, what is it?" I replied.

He put his hand on my back as he led me toward a table. "A lounge for those with more refined taste. I thought you'd like it."

I nodded and smiled. "I do."

My dress swished back and forth as Albert guided me toward a large table at the front of the room. A few men dressed in suits like Albert's sat playing cards. It seemed like an older game, not something that could be easily understood. They glanced up as we approached.

"Albert," the first one said, "you're back from America."

They embraced each other in the way men do. Moments later, they pulled apart. The man smiled at me and kissed my hand. I couldn't help but give him a small grin in return.

"Ms. Emerson," he whispered, "I've heard a lot about you."

"Though we didn't know how gorgeous you are," the other man added.

Albert rolled his eyes. "Don't scare her. She only got here yesterday."

"Have a drink, then," the first man said.

He handed me a tall glass full of blood. I could smell a hint of cherry mixed in with its familiar taste. I sighed, tilting it up to my mouth. It was fresh, cold, and thick. Albert took one and drank it, too. He smiled.

"Anne, dance with me?" Albert asked.

I laughed. "Isn't that a familiar question"

He took my hand, pulling me into the small circle of swishing dresses and soft breaths. I'd never been somewhere like this before. Perhaps this was why vampires chose to live in large covens. Albert had his own monstrosity of a clan back home. His mansion was a stronghold. This was almost the same. Everyone here had something in common. We could relate to each other.

But in the middle of it all, there was only one thing I really noticed. Albert was the most magnificent thing in the room. He had one hand on my back and the other around my waist as he pulled me toward him. The music was soft and slow, just the gentle sound of a piano. Albert's eyes bored into mine as he smiled. I placed a kiss on his cheek. He pulled me closer, planting his lips firmly against mine.

Perhaps I wouldn't go back to Savannah for a while. Maybe London, vampire-London, was just what I needed. This city was stuffed to the brim with magic. It felt natural to be here. The fog and chill gave it a mystical feel. It was appealing to me. I didn't seem so out of place.

Being here with Albert was like walking into a dream. Nothing seemed to be wrong. I could forget about James. Even my human life seemed to become insignificant. He filled every hole that threatened to make my heart fall apart. Kissing him was like falling into a bed of bliss. I never wanted to stop. Thankfully, I didn't have to.

This new world was enough to make my body feel warm. Tingling sensations flowed through me as I relished in the magic of it all. I was overcome with love, comfort, and thrill. How was it possible to be so calm yet thrilled at the same time? Only because of Albert did I feel safer than I ever had before. He made me feel that my world finally had order and peace.

As I looked up to admire his eyes, I let my body press against his. The silk of my dress was brushing up against his jacket. It was a gentle rub of smooth fabrics that blended together. They were like us. Albert and I became seamless, silken ribbons intertwined in a way that didn't fall apart. Together, we were a beautiful display of art in its finest form.

Chapter Nine

CENDRILLON

We came home late that night. Albert and I spent the early hours of the morning reading in each other's arms. Being curled up next to him in my giant, purple bed was wonderful. It felt like being wrapped in a blanket of love. His arms around me made me feel safe. They were a haven for my running mind. When I was laying against him, time stopped. I didn't have to think. All I had to do was feel. Albert cleared my mind like a warm cup of tea. The words he whispered in my ear made me melt. They were so powerful and overwhelming that they made me want to stay tucked in his arms forever.

He'd gotten up to answer a phone call. I decided to make good use of my time and take a shower. While he was downstairs talking about some boring business deal, I watched the soap travel down my arms and legs. The lavender shampoo was strong enough to overpower my senses. Rosemary oil coated my body with drops that made their way down my chest and onto my abdomen. I felt like a flower. The room smelled as if it were a garden. When I closed my eyes, I imagined I was walking through a meadow. Wildflowers sprouted around me as my dress swirled in the wind. But when I opened my eyes, I saw the pretty skylight above me that revealed the grayish-blue London air. Yet it didn't bother me. I was starting to love this place. The beaches weren't the same, but England had its own charms.

Albert was happy here. Of course, I hoped his change of mood had something to do with me. Still, I couldn't help but notice that he seemed more like himself in London. He didn't seem to feel the need to pretend. He was like a butterfly that had been set loose. When he reached England, he could finally fly. I didn't want to take him away from here. Besides, we were both happy. We literally had forever to decide where we wanted to live. There wasn't a reason we couldn't split our time between two places. But right now, I was happy in this foggy town.

I stepped out of the shower and wrapped my towel around my body. In the mirror, I looked like a creature of snow. My lips were bright red, my eyes sparkling blue, and my raven hair bunched in wet curls. I was Snow White, but not the Disney version. Perhaps a retelling of the classic tale in nightmare form. It wasn't a story for children.

I put on a purple dress that fell to my knees in a swirl of cotton. My feet were bare, and my toenails dark blue. A warm sweater was wrapped around my shoulders, making me look like a girl prepared for a cozy afternoon at home.

When I left the bathroom, I found a bundle of roses upon my bed. Their scent was intoxicating. I lifted one to my nose and inhaled its sweet aroma. Albert was a true romantic. He didn't appear to be, but on the inside, he was fully consumed with the gestures of love. Albert did little things like leaving me flowers to express his heart. It was precious.

I reached up to feel his necklace lightly laying against my throat. The little ruby was a drop of color upon my frozen form. Whenever I looked at it, I saw him. The phantom memory of his touch brushed against my waist as I stroked the silver chain. I loved him more than I wanted to admit to myself. Love is truly dangerous. Giving yourself over to someone is always a risk. But being with him, it made me feel beautiful again. Love does that sort of thing. It takes your insides and makes them all warm and tight. Just thinking about him, I felt the flutters in my stomach and the tightness in my abdomen.

I placed the roses in a vase beside my bed before going in search of Albert. I heard his voice on the first floor and descended to see him in the sitting room with Hazel. Though they were brother and sister, they looked nothing alike. Her straight, fiery red hair was a stark contrast to his brown curls. They were both pale, but that was to be expected. Her cheeks were flushed a rosy color, and her eyes were sharp like knives. Hazel was more than intimidating.

I wondered what she knew about me. Had Albert told her about us? She must have known something. Or maybe she thought I was just another one of his flings. If she knew the truth, she'd understand that he'd been pursuing me for years. We weren't a passing phase. It was something we'd had inside us for a long time. I'd pushed it away when I'd fallen in love with James. Because yes, it's very possible to be in love with two people at the same time. During those weeks, I'd had two men in my heart. Like most girls, I hadn't wanted to admit it. It's complicated to be in love with two men at the same time. It's easier to pretend you're not, to act as if your feelings aren't there. But now, my love for Albert was undeniable. Blocking it out would have been like telling the tides not to come in or the moon not to shine.

Hazel was sitting on the couch beside her brother. I hadn't paid much attention to the sitting room before. It was standard but elegant. It wasn't as personal as the other rooms. Perhaps this was where Albert spoke to his business partners. He didn't want to give them access to his life. Very few people had that luxury.

There was a small fireplace in the corner of the room. Flames were slowly erupting within it. It reminded me of where I was. It was fall in London, and that meant that it was cold. The leaves had just started to fall outside. Maybe we'd spend Christmas bundled up in this townhouse. I could even invite Nina, Anya, Arthur, and Roy. It would be my first Christmas with Albert. No matter what, I'd always remember it.

Albert's eyes met mine with a little smile. He beckoned me over to sit on his other side. Hazel's face was neutral. I couldn't tell exactly what she thought about me. It was probably some level of dislike, but I wasn't sure how deep.

She wore a blue dress that gripped her waist in a tight hold. Her body was pencil-thin, barely big enough to look adult. She looked slightly adolescent. Of course, she'd been older than Albert when she became a vampire. He'd been in his early twenties. Perhaps Hazel had only been a year or so older. Either way, she looked younger than me. That didn't make her less scary. I knew just how powerful she was. Hazel had a huge clan of her own. If Albert was a vampire prince, she was a princess.

"Hazel came over to extend an invitation," Albert said.

I raised my eyebrows. "To what?"

She gave me a stiff smile. "My annual Victorian ball."

Albert smiled at me. "I assume you want to go?"

I put my hand on his leg. "Definitely."

We had a moment of silent communication. Albert knew his sister wasn't a huge fan of mine. It was clear from the look in his eyes that this was a chance for him to show me off. He wanted me to go in there and steal the show. Of course, I'd do it for him. It was his idea that was traveling between us. Still, it would give me a small bit of satisfaction to walk in there and show them what a Georgia girl could do. This ball would be our big debut. Everyone would finally discover that Albert Jefferson had been taken off the market. I'd stolen his heart, and it would soon be the drama circling the supernatural side of London.

"Of course, it's tomorrow. So you'll have to find a dress," she added.

There was a look of superiority in Hazel's eyes. She had trapped me. I could hardly attend without a dress. And the ones in my closet wouldn't do. I needed a Victorian gown. Those weren't particularly easy to find.

Albert smiled. "Don't worry, I've got that covered."

I felt a sigh of relief escape my lips. It was one less thing to worry about. I already had to muster up enough courage to enter a ballroom full of vampires I didn't know. But Albert would be with me; that was enough.

She stood abruptly. "I'll be getting back, then. The people decorating can't seem to manage it."

Albert smiled. "We'll see you tomorrow."

She nodded before turning and leaving the room. As soon as I heard the click of the front door, I knew she was gone. I leaned back against the couch and let out another sigh of relief. Albert laughed and threw his arms around me.

I giggled. "Where's this mystery ball gown?"

He shrugged. "The dance is always at the same time every year. I ordered it ahead of time. It's in one of the spare bedrooms."

I grinned. "Can I see?"

He motioned to the stairs. "Lead the way."

I was starting to enjoy these little surprises. He always seemed to have something planned to make me smile. Albert enjoyed it, too. He had a look of satisfaction every time I smiled with excitement. It was almost like a little game we'd started to play.

I burst into the first spare bedroom with excitement in my eyes. Albert was right behind me as I ran over to the plain white bed with my dress laying atop it. I stopped for a moment. It was almost too much.

The dress was a deep navy blue color with white roses around the top and lace framing the edges. It was in the typical Victorian style, like the dresses I'd seen in paintings of the old South. Several of the portraits Albert had hanging throughout the house had women dressed in the same style. I knew how I'd wear it: with large hoops within my underskirts and white gloves that reached my elbows. It was the type of dress that little girls dreamed of wearing. Victorian England suddenly seemed very close to me. It was as if I could reach out and grasp the era of Albert's childhood.

"What do you think?" Albert asked.

"I can't wait," I replied.

He leaned down and placed a soft kiss below my ear. "I'll be honored to accompany you, Ms. Emerson."

I wrapped my arms around his neck, pulling his mouth toward mine. Our lips crushed against each other. He lifted me up as I wrapped my legs around him. His hands tangled in my hair as we fell against each other. This man was everything I wanted. He was my future. Together, we'd have a life.

He set me down, reaching behind him to retrieve a box that had been sitting on a chest near the end of the bed. It was larger than a box that would normally hold jewelry. I wasn't sure what it was. Of course, I'd wear the necklace he'd given me. It was an original from the time period. But did he have something else, too? What could it be?

"This is for you," he whispered.

I took the box from him. "What is it?"

He gently stroked my hair. "It was passed down in my family. Again, Hazel didn't want it. She kind of likes to do her own thing. Let's just say she has her own style."

I opened the velvet box to reveal something I'd never imagined. It was right there in front of me, yet it felt like a dream. He couldn't possibly be giving this to me. The necklace was enough. I didn't need more. He'd already given me a real, perfectly formed ruby. That was plenty. This was over the top. It was extravagant. But then again, so was Albert.

The surprise gift was a shining tiara of silver leaves embedded with tiny diamonds. It was more delicate than any piece of jewelry I'd ever seen, yet entirely powerful. I touched it carefully so as not to hurt the fragile leaves. It made me think of Shakespeare, or maybe even my own French past. The name Bourbon kept echoing in my mind. I belonged in this world. Albert's life of aristocratic bliss was in my ancestry as much as his. Together, we would rule this ball.

"You're going to be the Cinderella tomorrow night," he whispered.

I smiled. "Only because of you."

He grinned. "One day, I'm going to marry you, Ms. Emerson."

He hadn't bothered to say it like it was a question, and I was okay with that. My heart fluttered as his hands traveled across my elbows and up across my gentle shoulders. His eyes consumed my hips and upper legs. Who knew a glance could be so powerful? He could touch me with just his eyes. Yet, even so, this ghostly embrace was overpowering. I lost myself in his gorgeous smile. This was the world I wanted to live in. Albert had taken over my thoughts, and I was entirely happy about it.

Chapter Ten

PENELOPE JOY

I felt like a true Bourbon girl. Juli stood behind me, tightening the laces on my corset. It didn't hurt, but if I was human, it would have. The sensation of being stuffed into a wire encasement wasn't enjoyable. I felt like Jell-O. My chest was propped up in an awkward angle while my waist looked minuscule. My hips stuck out at the sides, allowing the wire hoops to hang gently from them. The outfit was genuine—it wasn't a fabrication. The dress had been made to be realistic. Tonight would feel as if I were stepping back in time. I'd be in Albert's world.

Juli had arranged my hair in an updo of intricate curls that looked as if it had come from a Jane Austen movie. Laced into the back of my hair were white roses to match the ones on the front of my dress. Set atop my hair was the tiara Albert had given me. I felt mystical, princess-like. This whole experience was magical. I reached up to touch the delicate choker around my neck. The ruby glimmered in the low light. It was about the same color as my painted lips. The only color on my face existed upon my mouth, eyelashes, eyebrows, and cheeks. I wore eyeliner, mascara, blush, and lipstick. There was a bit of blush on my cheeks, too. I was still pale, but I didn't mind.

Juli helped me slip the dark blue dress over my underskirts and corset. She pulled the back tightly closed, enclosing me within a shroud of blue and white lace. My hands were concealed in gloves that looked as if they belonged in a historical exhibit. They were so fragile I was afraid I'd rip them. Still, they slipped over my hands like silk.

When we had finished, I looked at myself in the mirror. In the candlelight, it looked so real. This little world I was stepping into felt genuine, like a time machine. Juli smiled from beside me as she adjusted my hair.

"I'm happy with my work," she said. "You're beautiful."

I smiled shyly. "Thank you for all your help."

She took my gloved hand within her own. "I'm happy he found you. I've been his housekeeper for a very long time. It's odd being an old woman for eternity. But this makes me content. It's a peaceful life. Albert was lonely for so long. I've never seen him so joyful."

I smiled back at her. "I love him so much."

She grinned before giving me a soft laugh. "I know, dear."

She turned away from me before walking out of the room. The door softly closed behind her as I was left to examine myself in my candlelit room. I only hoped to be pretty enough for him. I needed to be able to fit in at this party. I'd chosen a life with him, and now it was time to live it.

A soft knock sounded at the door before Albert entered. He wore the traditional Victorian Windsor outfit. His brown curls were tamed in a manner that allowed me a clear view of his dark eyes. Albert looked like he belonged in a fairytale. We both did. I allowed myself to look into the depths of his deep, mahogany soul. Albert's eyes collided with mine as he walked to me and placed his hand against my cheek.

"You are absolutely gorgeous," he whispered.

I looked up at him as he gently placed a kiss against my lips. He smelled like cherries and chocolate. The scent of sugar was everywhere. His hands were hard and cold as stone. Simply touching him was enough to make the butterflies in my stomach flutter.

"We'd better go," I replied.

He smiled before taking my hand to lead me from the room. This was going to be the biggest party of my life. For a few hours, I'd fall into a world of magic, beauty, and dream-like dresses.

~*~

For the first time in my life, I stuffed my skirts into a horse-drawn carriage. Hazel had ordered carriages for all her guests. Ours was pulled by two beautiful and majestic grey Irish draught horses. If I hadn't been so distracted by Albert, I would have stopped to admire them.

The ride wasn't too long. What felt like minutes later, Albert was helping me out into the night. The moonlight shone down upon our pale skin as we made our way up the path. At the end of the lane was a large Renaissance-style house surrounded by a garden of roses. Vampires of all ages, dressed in Victorian apparel, made their way into the mansion. As we walked, several of them glanced at us. Women's eyes were upon me as I held onto his arm. Soon, every vampire in the world would know who Albert Jefferson was with. And most likely, they'd be shocked.

When we entered the house, we stepped into a grand foyer. The carpet was cream colored and soft beneath my heels. Light emulated from the crystal chandelier above us. Albert held my hand as he led me down the hallway.

As soon as we turned the corner, I glimpsed the largest ballroom I'd ever seen. There were more candles than I could count, dresses swirling in gentle waves, and laughter rising to the ceiling. I felt as if I'd stepped into a fairytale. Albert wasn't paying attention to the scene, though. He was watching me. And moments later, so was everyone in the ballroom.

I held onto Albert's arm with incredible strength as we made our way through the crowd of gawking spectators. He had one of his characteristic smirks displayed on his face the whole time. Many of the guests looked at me with amazement, while others seemed to overflow with envy. A few of the women glared deeply with intense jealousy. It sent shivers through my body. They were practically bursting with anger. I'd have to get used to it. Many women all over the vampire world wanted Albert. For some bizarre reason, he'd chosen me. They would hate me for it.

I could feel every part of my body tense with the electricity that came from anxiety. The tight corset around my form, necklace upon my throat, and tiara on my head all seemed to catch my attention. I was aware of every piece of cloth on my body. My senses were on fire. I could feel everything. My fingertips were alive with energy as I held Albert's arm. I wanted to hide my fear, but it was difficult.

The sound of heavy breathing was everywhere. People shuffled to get out of our way as we moved through the path they'd created for us. After what felt like a very long journey, we finally reached Hazel. My anxiety certainly didn't flee at the sight of her. In fact, my chest grew stiff and heavy.

If I was Cinderella, she was Maleficent. The deep blue color of my dress was a stark contrast to her black gown. While I wore white gloves, she wore black. My lips were red, and hers were a dark purple. My chest was decorated with white roses, while hers was framed with lace. Her red hair was pulled into a layered updo with a Romanov-style tiara on the top of her head. She looked outlandishly beautiful. Hazel was gorgeous in the traditional gothic style. It was dark and mysterious. Others might say it was Dracula-like. Standing there across from each other, I was a daydream, and she was the picture of a sickeningly sweet nightmare. Only then did I realize that her hair was almost the shade of blood.

She smiled at Albert. "You came."

He kissed her hand. "You know I couldn't have stayed away."

She rolled her eyes. "I don't appreciate your neglect. It's been six months since you last visited."

He grinned. "You could always come to the States."

She shot him a deathly glare. "I've never been to America. Believe me, I don't intend on crossing the Atlantic."

"It's not as bad as you think, Hazel. You'd enjoy Georgia," he replied.

She smirked. "Perhaps."

A man with dark brown skin and a large smile approached to put his arm around her waist. Albert raised his eyebrows. He'd clearly never seen the man before. Hazel must have met him recently.

"Albert, this is Fredrick," she said.

Albert shook his hand. "It's nice to meet you."

Fredrick nodded. "It's nice to meet you, as well."

Suddenly, the music rose in volume. Albert placed his hand on my back and swept me away before I had a chance to greet Hazel's boyfriend. Though in a setting like this, the very terms "boyfriend" and "girlfriend" seemed odd. They didn't fit the time period. As the crowd of onlookers went back to their previous occupations, Albert began to pull me into a gentle waltz. I was glad that most of the vampires were no longer staring at me. The attention had been stressful. All I really wanted was to fall into Albert's arms. He held me against him, so I didn't have to look at anything other than his shoulder. It was a relief.

"What do you think of my sister's ball?" Albert asked.

"It's a little larger than I expected," I replied.

He laughed. "Hazel doesn't do anything halfheartedly."

I had no doubt about that. Everything was extravagant. She must have spent so many hours planning this. I wouldn't have had the patience for it. Perhaps living for over a hundred years gave someone a heightened sense of concentration. Albert certainly had persistence.

A waiter came up from behind me and offered me a glass of blood. Without paying much attention, I took it from him. Moments later, I smelled it. There was a slight scent of Champaign but also the unmistakable odor of human blood. I froze.

Albert leaned over to whisper in my ear. "Hazel doesn't follow our diet. About half the vampires here do, but she isn't like them. She refuses to try."

My jaw dropped. I was unable to reply. She seemed so sophisticated. I had never guessed that she drank human blood. Albert didn't seem bothered, though.

"She doesn't hurt people," he replied.

I nodded in acknowledgment. The blood was from a donor. No human had died at her hands. That was what I cared about. Still, I wouldn't drink it. It didn't feel right. The last time I'd sipped human blood had been when I'd changed James. I wasn't in the mood to relive that experience.

I placed the glass back on the tray. The waiter gave me a strange look but shrugged. Albert selected a different glass and handed it to me. Before I'd even brought it to my nose, I knew it wasn't human. Lamb's blood had a unique taste. I took a sip from the glass. Until the blood hit my lips, I didn't realize how hungry I had been. It felt good to relieve the strain in my throat. Moments later, I finished the glass. Albert kissed me before taking it from my hand and placing it back on the tray. The waiter, seemingly satisfied that he'd convinced me to drink something, walked away.

Moments later, I jerked to attention. The music had grown quiet again. Everyone was looking to the center of the room. Albert didn't seem to know what was happening either. He took my hand and pulled me further into the crowd.

We both froze at the same time. I'd never expected to see the scene before me. It was horrifying. Though no word had been spoken, I knew exactly what they were intending to do. I felt sick. The whole concept was disgusting. Nausea lifted in my stomach as if I had witnessed a grotesque accident. There was a rage burning in my heart that I knew I couldn't control.

Hazel stood in front of us with a baby, maybe five months old, in her arms. The little girl had blonde hair that looked like cornsilk and blue eyes that looked like mine. She was swaddled in a pink blanket. I could tell she was too overwhelmed to cry. She was in a state of shock.

Hazel laughed. "It's Fredrick's birthday, and I have a gift for him."

A few gasps went up around me. Some of the vampires stood in silence while others chucked or smirked. Albert seemed to be stunned. I grabbed his arm in an effort to get his attention. He looked back at me in understanding. We were both so stiff we could have been statues. This was a moment that truly felt like a horrific hallucination.

"I've never tried it myself, but I've heard it's ravishing," Hazel said. She traced a thin line across the baby's neck. "Honestly, I envy him."

I had to resist the urge to throw Hazel across the room and shove a stake through her heart. She wasn't intending to become a mother to this baby. No, she was planning something truly terrible. There was no way to describe it other than evil.

Fredrick stepped forward with hunger in his eyes. I felt as if I would collapse. Albert's hand was the only thing steadying me. I knew he wouldn't let it happen. Fredrick's fangs slipped from his lips. Terror flooded my heart. I was inwardly screaming.

Every nerve inside my body was burning. I wanted to wrap the girl in my arms and run. She deserved so much better. There was no way I could allow her to die. No, I would save her. Albert and I would bring her home.

Before Frederick had a chance to take the baby from Hazel's arms, Albert stepped toward them. "What do you think you're doing, Hazel?"

She rolled her eyes. "Oh, don't be so emotional. You're overreacting. Clearly, your diet has made you too sensitive."

A few chuckles sounded throughout the room, but Albert ignored them. "No, Hazel. Don't make this choice."

Hazel pursed her lips. "No one wanted it. The parents abandoned it on the side of the road. I didn't steal it from anyone."

Albert took a step forward. "It's not right, Hazel. Don't give up your humanity. She's a baby. You have no right to hurt her."

Hazel pulled the baby closer to her chest. "It was going to die either way."

Fredrick stepped closer to Albert with his fangs protruding from his mouth. "Give it to me."

A look of dominance crossed Albert's face. "I'm not going to let you hurt the baby."

Hazel looked just a little frightened. "Why are you being so dramatic about this?"

Albert extended his arms. "Give her to me now, or I will take her from you."

Fredrick attempted to step between them, but Albert shoved him away. Hazel looked terrified. Everyone in the room was too shocked at the unfolding scene to move. We all stood frozen with wide eyes. Not knowing what else to do, Hazel handed him the baby.

With inhuman speed, Albert was beside me again. I had just resumed breathing when he laid the baby in my arms and placed his hand on my back. I didn't bother saying anything. This was still too stunning for me to process.

"We're leaving," Albert whispered.

I wasn't aware of much of anything as I pressed the baby to my chest. She was soft against me. I had to be careful not to hurt her. Before I knew what was happening, Albert was lifting us up into the carriage.

The little girl was wrapped tightly in my shawl. Her soft heart gave little beats as she nestled within my arms. I could barely believe any of it was real. Even in my crazy world, I'd never dreamed of this.

Moments later, Albert was situated beside us as he told the driver to go. My mind was still spinning. I had intended to go to a ball with my boyfriend and his sister. The whole thing was supposed to have been a fun, relaxing evening. Instead, I had been struck with terror as I witnessed a room full of vampires drooling while relishing the concept of devouring a baby girl. Albert had saved her, and now we were on our way home with an infant.

As soon as we arrived at the townhouse, Albert ushered us inside. He firmly bolted the door behind us and sighed in relief. For a few moments, we stood there in silence. Our eyes drifted to the third person in the room. The tiny baby in my arms had fallen asleep. There was a peace about her that I never wanted to let go of. What were we going to do?

Without saying a word, Albert placed a hand on my back and led me up to the second floor. I sat on one of the couches with my skirts flaring out around me. Albert immediately picked up his phone and began talking to someone.

"Tom, there are a few things I need," he said. I heard a low mumble on the other end before Albert spoke again. "Diapers, formula, all the normal baby stuff. Don't ask questions. Please just have them here within the hour."

He set his phone on the table and sat down beside me. His eyes were focused on her. Mine were, too. We were both mesmerized. It was the first time I'd held a baby since I'd become a vampire. Her soft skin and little fingers were beautiful. I wanted to kiss her small head and never let her go. She was precious. This baby girl had been abandoned, and I resented her parents. They'd thrown away a precious gift. As an immortal, I could never have a baby. I envied the human girls who could. This child was a miracle, and she deserved love.

"Let me hold her," Albert whispered.

I gently set her in his arms. He cradled her like the most precious being on earth. Albert's eyes had never been so focused. In all the time I'd known him, I had never seen him so mesmerized. She slept peacefully in his arms. Like a little angel, the baby girl breathed softly with her lips parted in a tiny smile.

He brushed her blonde hair. "You're so pretty, Penny."

I raised my eyebrows. "Penny? How do you know her name?"

"I don't," he replied.

"Then why are you calling her that?" I asked.

"Well, what do you propose we call her, 'lunch'?" Albert asked in a tone dripping with sarcasm.

I pursed my lips. "That's not even funny."

He grinned. "It was kind of funny."

"Albert, this is serious!" I urged.

He rolled his eyes. "I'm aware of that."

Panic coursed through my voice. "What are we supposed to do with her?"

He looked at me in a matter-of-fact manner. "Well, Anne, we have two options. Option number one is that we move back to Savannah and dedicate the next eighteen years of our lives to this small human." He paused for a moment before a small grin crept onto his face. "Option number two is that we call the police and say, 'Officer, I need you to come to pick up this abandoned baby that my deranged, vampire sister was planning on feeding to her boyfriend, who obviously has emotional issues, for his birthday at a Victorian ball full of hundreds of similarly psychotic lunatics.'"

Though I tried my best, I couldn't help but laugh. He grinned at me as I smiled back. This was a ridiculous situation. How were two vampires supposed to take care of a baby? Still, we were probably better suited for the job than some human parents.

"What will we do about our ages? Not our real ones, but how we look. To any human, I look like a seventeen-year-old girl, and you look like you just got out of college. What will they think?" I asked.

He smirked. "That we need our own reality TV show."

At that, we both burst out laughing. The stress was too much. This was by far one of the most bizarre situations I'd ever gotten myself into. Albert and I, two vampires, had somehow found ourselves responsible for a baby girl. In about twenty minutes, we'd become parents.

Juli entered the room with a bottle in hand. She smiled in amazement as she gently placed the bottle in Albert's grasp. This baby girl had gone to sleep an orphan but would wake up as the daughter of one of the most powerful vampires in the world.

Albert smiled at me. "You should change. I'm sure that corset is killing you."

I groaned. "It's horrible."

He chuckled. "Go find something more comfortable, Momma. We'll be here when you get back."

My heart fluttered a little as I looked at the man I loved holding our daughter. It took me a moment to process the concept. Of course, I wouldn't fully grasp the situation for a while. But at the moment, all I could think about was that I had a baby girl.

Before I left the room, Albert spoke. "By the way, Penelope was my mom's name. That's what her first name will be, but we can call her 'Penny.' We still need to pick a middle name. I'm not sure what it should be," Albert said.

I smiled. "Joy. That's what her middle name will be."

Albert looked down at her. "Penelope Joy Jefferson, do you know that you have the most beautiful momma in the world?"

Chapter Eleven

HOME

After I'd relieved myself of the corset, taken my hair down, and changed into a pair of sweatpants and a sweatshirt, I returned to the second floor. Albert still wore his Windsor uniform. They looked like a perfect picture. He held Penny, still swaddled in a blanket, in his arms. It was a father-daughter moment I didn't want to interrupt. He smiled at her with eyes filled with pure joy. She was curiously aware as she drank her bottle, glancing up at him occasionally.

"Would you take her for a minute?" Albert asked. "I'd like to change."

It was such a mundane statement. How odd for a vampire to be holding a baby. People saw us as creatures of darkness, and there was some truth to it. But this, the fact that we'd just openly accepted a baby girl as our daughter, proved that we were more than blood-sucking monsters. Part of us remained human. I wanted my humanity to determine my actions. Even though I was destined to live my life as a child of the night, I wanted my heart to be filled with light.

I smiled. "Of course."

He reluctantly handed her over. For a moment, he stood there watching as I sat down with her. She continued to drink her bottle in a peaceful state of relaxation. Penny was a quiet baby. Her little form barely reacted as I pulled her closer to my chest. I was still processing the fact that within the last hour, I'd become a mother. Albert and I were parents. Though Albert and I had just begun our journey as a couple, we had already ended up with a baby. It was something that could have never happened naturally. Yet, even so, it was better than a dream.

I'd always wanted a baby, and now I had one. Of course, it had occurred in one of the strangest ways possible. Albert had to be traumatized. After all, he'd just watched his sister about to murder an infant. I knew he loved Hazel. But at the moment, he wasn't focusing on anything other than Penny.

I'd never known he had such a strong desire for a child. Of course, we'd both grown up in eras where having children was an integral part of life. It was ingrained into us just as the desire for blood was integral to a vampire. As much as our darker sides craved the fulfillment of drinking, our humanity hoped for a child. We finally had the missing piece of our immortal lives.

I heard his footsteps as he left the room. For the first time, Penny and I were alone. I touched her little nose with my finger and traced the outline of her little face. She was so incredibly soft. Her skin was more tender than a rose petal. She was so breakable that it scared me. It was as if I'd been charged with the protection of some precious artifact. I didn't want to let her out of my sight for a moment. In less than an hour, she'd stolen my heart.

When she finished her bottle, I set it off to the side. She wasn't ready to go back to sleep. Her little hand reached up to grab one of my curls. I watched as she explored its texture. Her tiny fingers tugged on it in a gentle pull. Our eyes met as she opened her mouth and gave a little giggle.

It seemed as if it had only been a few minutes

when Albert returned. He walked over and gently kissed my cheek. I leaned into him as he sat beside me and wrapped his arm around my shoulder.

"We need to go back to Savannah," he said.

I nodded. "I know." I paused for a moment. "Do you think Hazel will be furious with you?"

He let out a sigh. "I don't really have the energy to talk to her right now. I guess we'll have to see what happens. At the moment, I have more pressing priorities."

We both sat in silence for a few seconds as we watched Penny tug at my chest. She was exploring me. Maybe no one had ever really held her before. If they had, they certainly couldn't have loved her. Albert and I seemed to be the first people to care whether she lived or died. As a baby, Penny couldn't comprehend the scope of what had occurred. But in a few weeks, she'd start to realize who we were. Eventually, she'd never remember a time when we hadn't been her parents.

"Your sisters are already back in Savannah. They went back after we left for London," he said.

"What will we tell them?" I asked.

He sighed in exhaustion. "The truth."

I rested my head against his chest. "I love you, Albert."

"I love you too, little dove," he whispered.

~*~

We packed up our things and loaded onto the plane. I'd swaddled Penny in cloth wrap against my chest in order to keep her as close to me as possible. I was relieved when she finally fell asleep. She cried for a while after we boarded the plane. The takeoff had made her anxious. Albert had been absolutely panicked about what to do. I'd never seen him so nervous. Once she'd fallen asleep, we both relaxed.

This flight seemed shorter than our previous trip. Albert had been making phone calls in preparation for our arrival. Everyone on the other end seemed perplexed by his odd requests. After all, why would a vampire need to decorate a nursery? We would have a lot of people to explain this to. No one would let this slide. I didn't call Nina and Anya. It would be better to tell them in person. I wasn't really sure how to describe the situation, either. Albert would have to do most of the talking. They wouldn't be mad, just shocked. He'd be able to answer all their questions. I was still too dumbfounded to think about much of anything. I was focused on taking care of my baby. That was all I could manage.

When we landed, a car was waiting to pick us up. The driver didn't ask any questions, and I was glad about it. We'd have enough gawking stares when we arrived back at Albert's compound. This car ride was probably the last time we'd be alone for a while. I relished in the small moments as Albert held my hand while our baby was strapped to my chest. I didn't plan on letting go of her anytime soon. No one was taking her from my arms.

When we arrived home, Albert led me inside. The vampires in his coven stared blankly at us as we made our way toward the elevator. Expressions of shock and confusion were all around us. Albert silenced them with glares that made me nervous. He could be scary when he wanted to be. No one dared speak to us as we walked through the crowd.

I felt relief wash over me when the elevator doors closed behind us. I'd never been so anxious to get away from a swarming group of vampires. When we reached Albert's penthouse, I fully intended on locking the door behind us. This was not the time for questions that made my stomach turn upside down.

There was already too much craziness for me to worry about answering endless swarms of confused men and jealous women.

When we reached the top floor, we stepped out of the elevator into the little waiting area. Kara, Albert's secretary, was waiting for us in one of her signature suits. Her eyes grew wide for a moment before she recovered from her surprise. At this point, she was so used to Albert's strangeness that she barely even blinked.

"All of the baby things are inside," she said. "I tried to arrange it all exactly as you instructed."

Albert smiled at her. "Thank you, Kara."

He placed his hand on my back as he led me into his apartment and closed the door behind us. I heard the locks slide as he secured the penthouse from curious intruders. I let out a sigh of relief as he embraced me. Penny was clutched between us as he planted a kiss on my lips. It was tender and desperate. The stress of this situation was almost too much to handle.

"Well, it's time to inspect the nursery," Albert said.

I wasn't surprised that he already had it

decorated. Albert never paused. He was absolutely nonstop. He took my hand and pulled me down the hallway toward a room with a cream-colored door. As he opened it, I looked inside in absolute amazement.

A pale carpet that felt plush beneath my feet covered the floor. The walls were painted to resemble a fairytale forest. In the center of the room was a crib designed to look like a carriage. In the back was a large stuffed horse and a dollhouse. There was a bookshelf filled with classic fairy tales and poetry in the corner of the room illuminated by old-fashioned lanterns. And to top it all off, the ceiling was decorated with fairy lights.

"Is it all right?" Albert asked.

"It's wonderful," I whispered.

Albert led me toward the crib. "Maybe we should lay her down for a while."

I bit my lip. "Only for a few minutes."

He nodded. "Only for a few minutes."

As soon as I laid her down, he took my hand and pulled me back into the hallway. I gave him a questioning glance. He smiled back at me with one of his tell-tale looks. He had another surprise.

"I had a few changes made to our room to make it more agreeable to you. I want it to feel like ours," he said with a confident smile on his face.

Albert opened the door to reveal a bedroom beautiful enough to belong in a palace. I'd glanced in his room before, but this was totally different. In the center of the room was a large, French-style bed with grey upholstery and covers to match. Velvet pillows added splashes of pink to the elegant frame. I imagined laying in it with Albert beside me and Penny in my arms. We could read her fairytales as she drifted off to sleep. On either side of the bed were wooden nightstands that looked like antiques. They were a lovely match to the elaborate bed frame. Candlesticks sat atop them and flickered in the evening light. There was a window covered by curtains, a few bookshelves, and a little vanity lined with perfume. Of course, there was a closet too. Knowing Albert, it was probably already stocked with new clothes.

Laying upon the bed was a fresh bundle of baby's breath tied with a pink ribbon. I smiled softly to myself as I lifted it to my nose. Albert focused on every little detail. There was nothing he didn't consider. He was intent on making each moment as special as possible.

He sat down beside me as I slid my shoes off and reclined onto the bed. Albert wrapped his arms around me and pulled me close. His lips met mine in a gentle kiss that seemed to last for years.

"I want to try something," he whispered.

"What?" I asked.

He placed another little kiss on my cheek. "You'll see."

He repositioned himself against me with my lips above his neck. It took a moment before I realized what he meant. His dark eyes were earnest in their desire. He'd fed from me several times, but I'd never tried the same with him. The thought had never occurred to me before.

"You want me to?" I asked.

He nodded. "Very much."

I looked into his eyes for a few moments before giving him a gentle kiss and sinking my fangs into his neck. His arms wrapped around me and his hands tangled in my hair. I could feel his soft breathing as he began to relax. All logic left my mind as I delved into the world of bliss and blood. We were wrapped in a blanket of love as we closed our eyes and fell into perfect harmony.

Chapter Twelve
If I'd Never Loved You

Penny was wide awake and dressed in a pink jumpsuit. Her blonde hair was held back by a little headband and bow. She'd just finished her bottle and was ready to play. Albert held her while showing her a collection of plush dolls. I watched them while pacing back and forth on the hardwood floor as Albert's German shepherd, Cody, stared at me anxiously.

Nina and Anya were on their way. I'd called them an hour ago but hadn't told them exactly what was going on. They didn't know about Penny or that Albert and I were officially together. All they knew was that we'd returned from London.

I was a little nervous about telling them everything. What were they going to think? They wouldn't judge me, but I was afraid of how they might react. After all, I'd just come out of an intense relationship with James, who was now a vampire and nowhere to be found. I felt slightly responsible for that situation, but it wasn't completely my fault. He'd abandoned me, and there wasn't really anything I could have done to change it. Of course, I was thoroughly consumed with my love for Albert. My tumultuous love life had taught me a few things. Sometimes two people who were meant to love each other met at the wrong time. Perhaps James and I had loved each other in another life or universe. But at this moment, I was meant to be with Albert. James and I had experienced a great love, but it hadn't been meant to last forever. What I had with Albert was concrete. He was the permanent love of my life. It wasn't a choice. I couldn't run away from Albert. I'd tried it once, and all it had brought me was pain. When we were together, things fell into place.

We had a daughter now, too. Penny was the brightest star in my sky. She'd appeared out of nowhere but was here to stay. In only a few moments, my baby girl had stolen my heart. I could never let go of her. She made me remember my humanity.

There was a soft knock on the door as Nina and Anya swept into the room. Roy and Arthur followed closely behind. The girls moved to embrace me but stopped when they saw Penny in Albert's arms. The expressions on their faces went from shock to confusion as they looked at me in silence.

"Anne, why is there a baby here?" Nina asked. Her heels clicked on the floor as she moved to look into Penny's eyes.

Albert smiled. "Her name is Penny."

Nina raised her eyebrows. "Why do you have her?"

"And who gave her to you?" Anya asked.

Albert and I shared a glance before he spoke. "It's slightly complicated."

"Oh, don't worry, I'm more than ready for this undoubtedly dramatic saga," Nina replied.

The four of them sat across from us as Albert placed Penny in my arms. She cuddled close to my chest and began tugging on my hair. I reached down to pull a blanket around her. The girls kept giving me questioning glances.

"We rescued Penny from my disturbed sister, Hazel, who was planning on feeding Penny to her boyfriend. Apparently, it's become somewhat of a practice within certain European covens. After we saved Penny, Anne and I decided to adopt her," Albert answered.

They all looked absolutely horrified, surprised, and perplexed. Albert wrapped his arm around me as we waited for them to recover. This was by far one of the strangest discussions I'd ever had.

"So, you're together?" Nina clarified.

Albert smiled and placed a kiss on my cheek. "Forever."

A huge grin spread across Anya's face. "Finally."

Roy laughed. "I knew it was going to happen eventually."

"I need a drink," Arthur said.

Albert laughed before standing and leading the boys away. As they retreated to get drinks, Nina and Anya moved to sit beside me. They tenderly touched Penny with fascination. It was entirely odd to think that three vampire women were admiring a human baby. Then again, normal didn't seem to be a part of my life. There was nothing average about any of this.

"Can I hold her?" Nina asked.

I smiled. "Of course."

She carefully took Penny from my arms and began cradling her. Penny looked up at her with wide eyes filled with interest. She looked like a picture-perfect baby.

Anya laughed. "I guess you won't be moving back in with us."

I winked at her. "I'm a little preoccupied here."

We were all giggling when the boys walked back into the room. They carried six glasses of blood with them and one cup of puffs. I was so tempted to laugh. Albert Jefferson was holding a glass of blood in one hand, and baby puffs in the other. How had my life changed so quickly?

"So, no more late-night parties for the famous Albert Jefferson?" Arthur asked.

Roy laughed. "Anne finally calmed him down. The other girls will be fuming."

Albert smirked. "Don't worry, we'll get a babysitter."

He handed me a glass of blood before giving me a gentle kiss. Everyone was staring at us. The fact that we were openly displaying affection seemed to surprise them more than the knowledge that we'd adopted a baby.

"It's going to take a while to get used to that," Nina said.

Anya took Penny from Nina's arms. "It's my turn."

Albert took a sip. "I'm never getting my baby back. The aunts have stolen her."

He winked at me before standing to answer the classical phone on the other side of the room that was ringing incessantly. The boys still had slightly shocked expressions on their faces. Nina and Anya were consumed with Penny. We certainly had a village. Penny would be well cared for. None of us had expected to hold a baby again. Now that we had one to love, we certainly weren't going to take her for granted. I had a little girl of my own, and I wasn't going to forget how lucky I was.

It was only a few moments before Albert returned with a somber expression on his face. Something was wrong. I could see it in his eyes. Albert's lips were pulled into a tight frown as he ran a hand through his hair. Everyone grew quiet as we waited for him to speak.

"We have a problem," he stated.

"What is it?" Arthur asked.

Albert's eyes flickered to me before he replied. "While we were in London, a killing spree began here."

Everyone's faces grew white with shock. This happened sometimes, but not very much. Most vampires knew enough to conceal themselves. Killing randomly was a good way to alert the humans. Of course, vampires like us didn't kill at all. But the less conscious ones, those who didn't have self-control, sometimes went crazy. Their bloodlust consumed their personality. They became mindless killing machines.

"Do they know who it is?" I asked.

He looked at me with pity in his eyes. "James."

The world seemed to stop. Time was frozen still. I wanted to scream, cry, anything at all. But I couldn't because I was in too much pain. I had turned him. I had loved him. And I, because I'd fallen for a human, had caused this. It felt as if my heart had been tugged from my chest and stuffed into a shredder. It was absent from my chest. My porcelain body was still. My frozen eyes were focused on the glass of blood before me. I didn't feel alive. In that moment, I felt very, very dead.

"It's not your fault," Albert whispered.

"Albert's right, Anne. James makes his own choices," Nina added.

Anya nodded. "You didn't cause this."

"We'll take care of it for you," Arthur said.

Roy stood up to stand beside him. "You don't need to see this."

I shook my head. "No, I need to be the one to do it."

"Anne...," Albert whispered.

"No, Albert," I said softly. "I have to do this. I created him, and I need to end him."

Albert nodded. "All right, but I'm going with you."

"Us too," Arthur said.

I looked at the girls. Penny was sitting quietly with them as she pulled on the arms of a stuffed toy. I wanted her far away from this. She needed to be safe. No matter what else was happening in my life, she was my concern. I would deal with James, but only as long as I knew she was safe.

Nina and Anya had grim expressions on their faces. "Will you keep her?" I asked.

They smiled slightly. "Of course," Anya replied.

Albert took my hand in his. "It's time to get ready."

Chapter Thirteen

GOOD MEN FALL

I stared at myself in the long mirror. My black curls were pulled into a ponytail at the base of my neck. Leather adorned my stone body. Black pants, a skin-tight shirt, and combat boots made up my attire. I looked like a warrior, or maybe just a girl who was scared of what she was about to do.

I had to kill my ex-boyfriend. Not because I hated him or was angry with him. No, it was because he was killing people. I'd literally saved his life. When he was dying in my arms, I'd changed him. But when he'd woken up as a vampire, he'd lost both his memory and humanity. All the kindness he'd once possessed had vanished. Instead, he'd become a mindless killing machine. James had gone so far that he had to be ended. And though I didn't want to do it, I had to be the one to end his immortal life.

He had been my love. I adored him, fed him, and fought for him. When his life had been in danger, I had been prepared to sacrifice my life for his. There had been so much emotion packed into just a few weeks. But it had been a mistake. Honestly, I shouldn't have changed him. Then again, it had been out of love. How did I weigh the worth of dozens of lives he'd taken against the passion I had felt for our future?

"Are you ready?" Albert asked.

He wore jeans, a hoodie, work boots, and a leather jacket. His face was grim, with serious eyes. I wanted to fall into his arms and cry. That wasn't an option, though.

I didn't want to see James. In fact, I never wanted to think about him again. Perhaps after today, I wouldn't have to. Maybe after this was over, my heart would feel free. I could truly let him go. At least when it was over, he'd be free, too. His soul would leave this world. When he was transported to the afterlife, I had faith that the pureness of his heart would be restored.

I was doing him a kindness. If we'd discussed

this situation when he was human, he would have wanted me to end him. James had never wanted to hurt people. He'd wanted to live in peace. I'd never seen him be anything but kind. James had loved with such a passion that he would have moved mountains for me. If I'd asked him to, he would have taken on a hundred men all alone to protect me. He'd been a truly good man. When he was human, James had been the real-life version of Steve Rogers.

"Yes," I whispered.

Albert placed his hand on my back. He was my real-life Tony Stark. What a change I'd made. From Captain America to Iron Man. Who was I? Of that, I wasn't sure. I didn't know where I fit in this imaginary world I'd created. Maybe I was no one. Perhaps, in the end, I was just Anne Emerson. At this point, I was starting to become okay with just being me. But today, it was more difficult. Thinking of what I was responsible to do in a matter of hours was too terrifying.

"You don't have to go if you don't want to, love," he whispered.

I sighed. "I have to do this."

He nodded. "I understand."

His hands were on my waist as he pulled me toward him. Moments later, my arms were around his neck as he kissed me. The taste of his lips against mine made me forget James. For a brief moment, the only thing in the world was us. Every time his lips touched mine, I wanted to forget myself. When we were connected, he was my sole focus. Albert was my king, my shining star. We were a power couple. Together, we made the world shiver.

"I love you so much, angel," he whispered.

"I love you, too," I mumbled back.

The sun was shining on our porcelain bodies. We were beautiful creatures of the night, illuminated by the light of day. It was time to go. If we stayed for even minutes longer, another life might end. We had to take care of James before he hurt anyone else.

"It's time to leave," he said.

"I know," I replied with a sick feeling in my abdomen.

He led me toward the door. Before we left the room, I grabbed a wooden stake from the nightstand and stuffed it in my pocket. It felt heavy, almost as if it held the weight of the world.

I took a deep breath. "I'm ready."

Chapter Fourteen

DAGGER

The sun was beginning to set as we began our quest to find James. Though Roy and Arthur had ceased to be werewolves when they became vampires, they were still skilled at tracking. All evening they'd followed the scent of James, and his victims, across Savannah. Albert and I went with them as they were immersed in their tracking experience. It didn't take long before we discovered his location. He was staying in an abandoned building downtown.

It was in absolute disrepair. The ceiling was falling in, and the walls were collapsing. The floor was a cracked mess of dirt and wood. It looked like a scene from a horror movie. Could he have found anywhere more stereotypical for a monster to hide? Short of Dracula's castle, probably not.

We walked carefully as the boys followed James's scent to the top floor, a trail of blood leading the way. He wasn't even attempting to clean up his destruction. James must have gone completely off the deep end. He had always been so put-together and well-groomed. Now there was blood all over his nightmarish residence.

Albert's hand was on my back as we climbed the stairs to the top level. We walked so lightly that even a vampire couldn't hear our footsteps. Arthur gave a signal for us to move forward, and we continued our ascent.

When we finally reached the top floor, we were greeted by a heavy wooden door that was falling off the hinges. Years ago, it may have been sturdy. Now it looked like it would fall apart if we tried to open it.

"He's in there," Arthur whispered.

Roy nodded. "I can smell all the blood."

"What do we do?" I asked.

They all looked at me. "You're the boss," Albert said.

I took a deep breath before motioning toward the door. Arthur took that as his cue to go. Moments later, the door collapsed onto the ground after Arthur and Roy kicked it with their vampire strength. I dashed into the room with Albert behind me, only to run straight into James.

I took a few seconds to breathe, taking in his filthy form. I could feel the tears rolling down my cheeks. Even after all the mental hoops I'd jumped through, I hadn't been able to prepare myself for this. His once-blond hair was matted to his forehead with sweat and blood. James wore a plain T-shirt and jeans, but they were covered in the dried blood of his victims. His hands were stained with dirt, and his fingernails turned black.

"Anne?" James asked.

There was confusion in his eyes. He really didn't know why I was there. Maybe he truly believed he hadn't done anything wrong. But how was that possible? How could he have lost so much of himself? This wasn't the James I'd fallen in love with. He had ceased to be the sweet human boy who brought me roses. Instead, he'd become a terror.

"How many people have you killed?" I screamed, with tears dripping down my face.

But before he had a chance to respond, a gasp went up around the room. We all turned to look at another vampire we hadn't accounted for. In fact, we hadn't known she existed. Not as an immortal, anyway. This was a girl I'd known. I'd talked with her, shopped with her, and laughed with her. She was Roy and Arthur's sister, Darcey.

James must have changed her. That was the only answer to the question as to how she'd become a vampire. When we'd left Savannah, she'd been a werewolf like her brothers. It was incredible that James had managed to pick her for his vampire sidekick. This made the situation so much more complicated. She, like James, was covered in blood. Her hair was filthy and matted to her torn dress. She looked like she'd crawled out of a grave.

"Darcey...," Arthur whispered.

Roy stood silently as he watched his sister with horror. How could we react to this? Now there were two people in this room we loved but had to kill. They both looked like monsters. But even so, did I have the heart to do it? And even if I could kill James, what would we do about Darcey? We had no idea how she'd gotten wrapped up in all of this.

Roy flew across the room to James and pinned him against the wall. "What did you do to my sister?"

"She wanted it," James hissed. "After she saw how amazing it was, she begged for it."

"You better do it fast, Anne, or I'm going to," Roy growled.

"Do what?" James asked.

Albert sneered. "Drive a stake through your pathetic heart."

Darcey screamed. "No!"

Arthur grabbed her from behind and held her against him. Darcey struggled against his grip but wasn't strong enough to push her brother away. He held her with a fierceness that she wouldn't be able to escape from.

James looked at me pleadingly. "Aren't you supposed to be in love with me? I thought that was what this was all about. Didn't you turn me so we could be together forever? What happened to that love, Anne?"

He was trying to manipulate me. None of this was what he honestly felt. At this point, his emotions were buried too deeply to make a reappearance any time soon. This was a survival mechanism. All he was doing was trying to make me freeze. He wanted a chance to escape. Perhaps he knew that Albert wouldn't do something against my will.

I shook my head. "I don't love you anymore."

James was still trapped in Roy's hold. "So you'll kill me because you lost feelings? Or are you jealous of Darcey? Is that it?"

It was a low blow. He was lashing out in anger. It was fear that was controlling him. It was all too clear. He underestimated me. James took me for a helpless girl, but I wasn't. After years and years of immortal life, I was a woman capable of doing the unimaginable. I could kill, but only in situations like this. I had to end his life to prevent the deaths of innocents. He was a homicidal serial killer. This couldn't go on. If we let him keep killing people, it would be our fault. At this point, killing him was the only choice I could make that would free him from his own murderous mind.

I wanted to scream. Teardrops were still dripping down my cheeks. "No, James! It's because you're killing people. You're throwing human life away like it's trash."

He laughed. "It is, Anne! That's what they're here for. We need to feed. It's who we are."

I hardly wanted to believe this was real. He was

truly becoming the nightmare I'd wanted to avoid. Maybe it was better not to focus on the negative aspects. It was hard to deal with the memory, though. Continual reminders of the former James were all over my skin, like a layer of ice I couldn't shake.

Mascara was running down my face, along with my eyeliner. "You're a monster."

James smirked. "Said Bram Stoker to Dracula."

"Enough!" Roy screamed.

His face had gone totally red. The anger in his eyes was continuing to build. Albert stood beside him with the same amount of contempt in his eyes. Arthur was still holding Darcey, who was sobbing in his arms.

I walked up to James with my stake in hand. When he saw it, he seemed to finally process what was going to happen. I'd only ever killed one other vampire before: the man who'd turned me. It had been out of pure fury and rage. I'd felt no remorse for ending his life. But this, I wouldn't be able to forget it for the rest of my immortal life.

"Remember, I'll do it if you don't want to," Albert whispered in my ear.

I took his hand in my own. "It's okay. I should

be the one to end it."

"Please don't hurt him," Darcey cried. "I love him!"

I raised my eyebrows. "You barely know who he is."

James rolled his eyes. "The girl falls fast."

"Say one more word, and I will end you," Roy growled.

The only thing that had stayed consistent about James was his emerald eyes. When he had been human, they had held so much love. Now they were covered in darkness, but still so beautiful. Part of me wanted to try to pull him back. And maybe if I had been a stronger person, I would have tried. But I wanted to put James out of his misery.

I felt the wooden stake in my hand. It was heavy and cold, dark and ominous. I felt like I was in a horrible movie. It was literally the opposite of *Romeo and Juliet*. This had to be a dream because it couldn't be real. There was no way my love life was this catastrophic.

"You'll really do it, huh?" James whispered.

"I can't let you keep hurting people," I replied.

"That's all right," he sneered. "I'd rather die

feeling alive than be the weak, sickening version of an immortal you are."

With one final look into his eyes, I drove the stake into his heart. I didn't know what to expect. Since I'd only ever seen one vampire die, and in a far less delicate way, I had no idea how it worked. Honestly, it was quick and simple.

His eyes fogged over before his lips turned white, and his body became inhumanly still. Soon after, his skin became grey and started falling to the ground in flakes. I watched as the man I'd once loved melted into ash. He was falling into nothing. In the distance, I could hear Darcey screaming. It sounded like she was a million miles away. I was too focused on watching James blow into the wind.

My knees hit the ground as I landed beside his melting body. At this point, my hair had fallen around my face in a jumbled mess of chaos. My face was stained with makeup and dripping with tears. I looked like an absolute disaster, but it didn't matter. All I could feel was a stabbing pain in my chest. I felt as if I was choking on air. The very floor beneath me seemed to shake. My vision was going blurry as the wave of emotions rushed through me. Albert was beside me with his hands on my back, but I couldn't hear anything he was saying. The world had gone dark.

In a moment of distraction, Darcey escaped from Arthur's hold and dashed toward me. She tackled me to the ground and began snarling at me. She seemed like a rabid animal. In her current state, she was far more animal-like than the werewolf she'd once been. This was the crazy type of vampire ancient people had been scared of. Humans in centuries past had been terrified of vampires like this. Darcey was a creature far different than us. She wasn't civilized.

When I looked into her eyes, I saw horrific pain. She hated herself. There was a part of her that was still the Darcey she'd once been. Even so, we couldn't save her. She had to choose that for herself. And at the moment, the only thing she was trying to do was kill me.

"You killed him!" Darcey screamed.

Not more than a moment after she'd pounced on me, Albert pulled her back and threw her against the ground in a blind rage. Roy and Arthur grabbed her arms and held her down. She was snarling and screaming beneath them.

This wasn't what I'd wanted. I'd never planned on anyone else getting hurt. But Darcey, in her blood-stained dress and makeup-smeared face, was in pain. Whether or not she'd actually wanted to become a vampire, it had clearly been a mistake. She was filled with pent up rage, and none of us knew how to help her.

Arthur and Roy shared a brief glance that seemed to speak volumes. Before Albert or I had the chance to say anything, they pulled a piece of wood from the fractured floor and shoved it through her chest. Like James, she fell into a pile of grey flakes that turned into nothing. In mere minutes, we'd ended two lives: my ex-boyfriend's and their sister's. There weren't even bodies to bury. It was just ash, pieces of dust that melted into the shadows.

The room was completely silent. Not one of us moved. There was a bit of blood streaked across my cheek, but it wasn't mine. It belonged to one of James's victims. We were all stained with blood from the clothes of the two vampires we'd just killed. It was as if we'd escaped from a battle. Though I looked like I'd just won a war, I certainly didn't feel like it. Everything inside me was falling apart.

"We should get you home," Albert whispered.

Arthur and Roy were in too much of a daze to do anything but follow as Albert lifted me from the floor. He held me tightly against him as we left the desolate building to flee from the scene. I never wanted to return to this place. In fact, I wanted to leave Savannah. I didn't want to be in Georgia anymore, not after this.

The moon was bright in the sky when we arrived back at Albert's apartment. None of us had said a single word on the drive back. Arthur and Roy hadn't even fully processed the events. I could tell by the glossy looks in their eyes that nothing seemed real anymore.

Nina and Anya greeted us as we walked into the living room. They didn't say anything as Albert took my hand and led me toward our bedroom. After Albert closed the door behind us, he picked me up and placed me on the bed. The grey covers were soft and cool beneath my fingers. I felt as if I were sinking into an ocean made of cotton.

Albert stroked my cheek. "I'll start a bath."

And with that, he left me alone to ponder the death of my ex-lover. The room was dimly lit. As I lay thinking of the life I'd just taken, I wasn't sure whether or not I was the monster.

Chapter Fifteen

Eros

While I was taking my bath, Albert had explained the situation to Nina and Anya before sending them home with the boys. I was sure they were all panicking, but Albert told me not to worry about it. He said I had enough on my plate. Besides, he assured me that he would take care of everyone. And he would because that's what Albert did. He managed things in times of stress. At the moment, I didn't have the energy to worry about anything else. Stabbing a dagger through James's heart had been bad enough. I just couldn't deal with more. Nina and Anya would take care of Roy and Arthur. They'd survive this.

I emerged from the bathroom to find Albert sitting on our bed in a pair of blue sweatpants. I felt silly in my frilly nightgown. The purple silk felt absolutely ridiculous. I'd just killed a man. My hair was still a wet, tangled mess, and I had just finished clearing the smudged eyeshadow from my face. I smelled like roses, but only because I'd had to dump the body wash all over me to scrub away the blood.

He must have showered in the other bathroom because he was no longer covered in blood and dirt. His hair was back to being an assortment of jumbled curls that looked lazy as they fell against his forehead. His eyes, though tainted by the horror of what we had experienced, were still a deep, mysterious ocean. At that moment, I wanted to become a part of him. I no longer cared what was healthy or if this was insane. Albert was all I could see.

He looked up at me with a gaze that seemed to penetrate my body. Everything about him seemed more intense than usual. His lips were pursed in a tight line that held anxiety. Albert looked as if he might fall apart. I was glimpsing the very carefully crafted shell that surrounded his heart.

I sat down on the bed beside him. Suddenly, I was aware of so much. His shoulders were far more shaped than I had once thought. The jaw that held up his smirk was firm and strong above his neck. His chest, while pale and stone-like, was more toned than most. Though he wasn't smiling, his arms seemed to invite me in. I leaned over to place my head against his shoulder.

Without hesitation, he wrapped his arms around me. I felt his strong hands press against my waist as he pulled me closer. Unexpectedly, tears began to drip down my cheeks. I'd thought I blocked the emotion out. I wanted to be able to deal with this in the morning. It would take me so long to process everything that had happened in just a few short days. But as I felt the protective press of his chest against mine, I knew it was okay. I was sure I didn't have to be strong because he was strong for me.

In most cases, I liked to feel in control. It was easier to pretend I was the one in power. But with Albert, I was okay with just existing. The fact that I was alive, at least kind of, was enough. He didn't ask me to be perfect or even extraordinary. All he wanted was for me to be able to relax in his arms. Albert thrived on taking care of me. I wished I'd realized it earlier.

"It's not your fault," he said in a gentle tone.

"I feel like it is," I mumbled into his chest.

He sighed. "I know."

The tears kept dripping from my eyes. "I saw his eyes before I stabbed him. I won't ever be able to forget the way he looked at me."

"You did the right thing," Albert whispered.

"Did I?" I asked.

His fingers bored into my hips. "He was killing people, Anne."

I bit my lip. "I've killed people, too."

Albert shook his head. "He was too dangerous."

"I'm a monster," I cried.

He placed a gentle kiss on my hair. "You are not a monster."

"How am I any better than him?" I asked in a hushed tone.

Albert took a deep breath. "You try so hard. Anne, you love people. Without a moment's hesitation, you took Penny as your own. James had something wrong with him. His lack of empathy was like a disease. He didn't feel anything. James took human life carelessly. Anne, you feel so much that I sometimes worry the heaviness might tear you apart. You don't want to hurt anyone. James wasn't like that. Maybe he was as a human, but not as a vampire."

"I'm scared," I whispered. "What if I can never forget it?"

He squeezed me. "You won't be able to forget it, love. Your heart is too big for that. In time, you'll come to live with it. Tonight, another woman gets to live because James won't be there to destroy her. Another teenage boy gets to go home because Darcey won't be able to kill him. That's the legacy today's actions have left."

We laid there in silence for several more minutes. I just wanted to mesh into him. There was so much I had to make sense of. For once, there seemed nothing I could do. I couldn't go apologize to James's body. It didn't exist. In fact, there was nothing left of him. No grave, no coffin, no headstone. All I could do was remember his emerald eyes. But when I imagined them, I saw the way he'd looked at me before I killed him. Nothing was peaceful.

"I love you," I whispered.

Albert smiled softly. "I love you, too."

I leaned up against him to press a kiss to his lips. Until that moment, I hadn't realized how perfect he was for me. Albert was the steadiness I needed. Regardless of how reckless he appeared, he was grounded. Albert leaned back and pulled me down against him. He placed gentle kisses along my jaw. I breathed him in, smelling nothing but soap and salt.

My fingers traced his curls while his hands stroked my back. I wanted his love. Because after all of it, I'd found the one for me. This crazy love triangle was over. Albert was all-consuming. He didn't give me a moment to be distracted from his love.

I wanted this to be forever. With Albert, I could live semi-peacefully as an immortal. There was nothing stronger than my desire to be tied to him. I wanted to become so closely linked that we could never be separated. Albert was my choice. I would choose him over and over again until one day when we became so attached there was nothing to think about. He was going to be the love of my life. That was the role I was placing him in. This man that had once made me feel insecure and doubtful was now the only one I wanted. Albert held every part of me that I could possibly give away. And it was okay because I knew he would take care of me.

So in that moment, I let it all fall away. I didn't

want to fight anymore. This natural love was too strong to deny. We were exactly right for each other. It was a true, deep desire for happiness that brought us together in this swirl of need. My desire to have more of him would never end, and that was exactly how I wanted it.

Chapter Sixteen
SWEET FAREWELL

Penny rested gently in my arms as I rocked her in the low morning light. Her soft blonde hair was glowing in the sunlight. When she was sleeping, she looked like a doll. Her tiny fingers and toes fascinated me. How could anything be so small? What made her so angelic? I was still processing the knowledge that I'd become a mother. The concept was strange. I wished I'd had nine months to prepare.

James was dead. I didn't like thinking about it. The words couldn't seem to escape my mouth. No matter how hard I tried, it was almost impossible to acknowledge it. I felt like he might walk into the room at any moment. It had started to feel like a dream. The whole event was like a nightmare I couldn't get over. His face seemed to be in the corner of my vision, no matter where I looked. Would I ever get past it? Was it possible to forget killing a man you'd loved? There weren't many people I could ask about it. After all, it wasn't a particularly common experience.

Albert seemed to be giving me my space. He was working a lot but always accessible. He wasn't going out as much as normal. Actually, he hadn't spent even one evening away. Every night he was with me. I needed him, too. The girls were preoccupied with Roy and Arthur. They hadn't handled the loss of their sister well. Of course, how could they? There was no easy way to deal with trauma so terrible. Albert and I were focusing almost all our energy on Penny. She occupied our time. Taking care of her was the distraction I needed.

Still, Albert and I had the chance to enjoy a few stolen moments. They were the moments when all I could see were his eyes. When he kissed me, I wanted to disappear into his arms. Sometimes I just wanted to melt into him. The concept gave me a warm feeling in my abdomen. It was a familiar tingling at this point. I had stopped being surprised by the reaction that Albert's name elicited within me. He was just that right for me. I had more chemistry with him than I'd thought was possible. For so long, I hadn't known that two people could be so thoroughly linked together. He was my new definition of romance.

"I'm home," he whispered from the door.

I smiled slightly without turning around. Within a moment, his arms were around my waist. I leaned my head back against his shoulder as his lips planted soft kisses along my neck. A small sigh escaped my lips as he nuzzled his head against mine.

"I love you," he whispered.

"I love you too," I murmured back.

When I opened my eyes, I froze. James was standing right in front of me. I clutched Penny to my chest. My breathing had stopped altogether. James's green eyes were right before me. He said nothing yet stared at me with an intensity stronger than I imagined possible. He was the human James. This version of him had soft, silky skin. His hair was combed back in the organized fashion he'd always preferred. And his smile, it was gorgeous.

My body had tensed so much that Albert had noticed. "What's wrong?" Albert asked.

James smiled softly before lifting a finger to his lips. He shook his head and blew me a small kiss. My throat had grown tight. My whole body was on edge. It seemed that the world had become still. Penny was still motionless in my arms. Albert was waiting for my response.

James didn't want me to tell him, though. I could honor that, at least. I'd failed to keep him alive, but at least I could give him this one small thing. In that moment, he was my James. This was the human boy I'd been in love with, not the blood-drunk vampire running around on a killing spree. His smile widened again as he realized I was going to grant his request.

"Anne?" Albert asked.

I didn't know what was going on. Was I hallucinating? Was I dreaming? Were ghosts real? Nothing was out of the realm of possibility. After all, I was a vampire. Whatever it was—whatever James was—I was glad he was here. Just his small smile was enough to ease the heaviness within me. His spirit was comforting me. He was relieving me and assuring us both that it was all right. It gave me a small smile. We weren't in love, but we shared memories. It was a bond that ensured our permanent connection.

"It's nothing," I replied with a gentle smile. "Everything's fine."

Chapter Seventeen

To Our Forever

My new desk was made from dark wood and delicately shaped as if it had come from a historical exhibit. There were wooden pens with intricate designs carved into them and stationary decorated with flowered corners. Albert had stocked it with everything I could possibly need for letter writing.

I was writing another letter to James. I'd written one when he was in his transition. Of course, he'd never read it. The letter was still hidden away down in Texas. James would never receive this letter, either. I had a habit of writing letters to people who would never read them. They were more for me than anyone else. My words held secrets, confessions, and dreams. These letters were phrases whispered that could never be heard.

This letter was just one piece of the puzzle needed to stitch my life back together. I had to mumble the words in some way, even if it wasn't out loud. James and I had a long history of hushed phrases. This letter would just be another one of them. I was really going to have to start a journal. It might work a little better.

James,

I'm sorry. I really, truly regret what happened to you. Maybe loving you was right, or maybe it was terribly wrong. Either way, it led to this. You're dead. You're actually dead this time. It's not temporary. In fact, it feels very, very real.

I'm not sure what I regret. All of this led to where I am. I'm a new person, James. And I know you're finally at peace. I saw that familiar, human smile. Whatever happened to you, it made you happy again. Your humanity is back. I hope you are in a peaceful place. That's what I wish for you.

I have no idea how long this immortal life will last, but I may see you again. I'm not sure how it'll work, but maybe you'll come back. I'd like to see you live a human life. You should have fallen in love with a normal girl, gotten married, and had kids. That's what I wanted your life to look like.

Eventually, there might be a chance for you to have what you deserve. If somehow you come back, I want you to find me again. Just to say hello, or maybe goodbye. Either would be fine. We could part on positive terms. Because no matter what, I'll never be able to forget the memory of us. I don't feel the same way anymore. I'm completely in love with Albert. But even in a hundred years, I'll still remember you.

Some things can't be eliminated. The feel of your touch will fade into a million little pieces of sensation that I'll lose. But the sensation of your name on my tongue won't go away. Not love, just companionship. You made me feel joy again.

Have a peaceful forever, James. I'll remember you for the rest of my life and my existence after that. You were a great love of my life.

With love,
Anne

Albert was going to get a letter, too. He wasn't going to read it, either. These letters were both going to be placed under our bed in a box that I wouldn't open for at least ten years. After that, it might be a hundred more years before I opened it again. Maybe I'd stop opening it at some point. The box might get so dusty from neglect that I never wanted to touch it.

But for this moment, these pages were what was helping me hold on. I needed these words. The chaos, the disaster, all of it could be transfused into a few pages. I couldn't forget all of this, but I could write it down. Pouring my words onto the page helped me to remember how lucky I was that I was the woman who held Albert Jefferson's heart.

To the most important man in my life,

Thank you. I am so glad you never gave up on me. Through all our challenges, you never stopped trying to show me your love. Now we get to experience a love that will last many lifetimes. And I'll never be able to tell you how much I adore you.

Thank you for loving me and for taking care of this. You gave me a life and helped create a family. I'll happily live this immortal life with you because there's no one I'd rather spend my time with. You are the best lover, the best man, and the best partner of my existence.

We have Penny, our little girl. And there is nothing,

no way I would prefer to spend the next eighteen years of my life than raising her with you. Who knows what she'll decide to be. Maybe she'll stay human and live a wonderful life. But if she decides to become an immortal, we'll be with her every step of the way.

We created a life for ourselves. I love you more than I can express. So, love, I'm going to be yours forever. We have the rest of our lives to experience the beauty of this world. I am so ready to become your wife and forever companion.

Forever your love,
Anne

Chapter Eighteen
ETERNAL

The moon was brighter than it normally seemed. Penny was in a little baby basket with a big bow in her hair. She was sleeping quietly with a contented smile on her face. I couldn't stop admiring her sweet little features. I never wanted her to grow up. Why couldn't she stay a baby for the rest of forever? Then we would never have to worry about what we'd do when she was older. But right now, I had to enjoy her innocence. For at least a few more years, she would still be a little girl.

For the first time in days, I'd taken the time to do my hair. The curls that generally fell freely down were piled up in a bun upon my head. A sparkling silver pin tucked them together. Eyeliner and mascara highlighted my blue eyes. My lips were as red as a velvet cake. It was just another one of the days where I was positively sure I belonged in the live-action Snow White.

My green dress was more frilly than I usually liked. Albert had picked it out. The lace framed my hips, waist, and chest. My favorite part was the boots, though. They were black velvet and tall enough that they reached my knees. My nails were the same deep green color. Albert had told me to dress up tonight. We were having dinner while Nina and Anya watched Penny.

"The babysitters club has arrived," Nina called from the door.

I smiled before turning around. "Reporting for duty?"

Anya grinned. "One of the best jobs I've ever had."

"Let's hurry up, ladies," Albert said from the bedroom door. "Reservations can't be delayed."

Nina rolled her eyes. "He literally never stops."

"I heard that," Albert responded.

He walked up behind me and wrapped his arms around my waist. I leaned my head back against his shoulder. His lips lightly grazed my neck. I laughed as his fangs slipped from his lips.

"Okay, go," Anya said. "Seeing you two like that is still weird."

Nina and Anya both laughed. Albert rolled his eyes as he took my hand and pulled me away from them. Nina winked at me, and Anya smirked as Albert closed the door.

As soon as the lock slid shut, Albert pulled me against him. Our lips locked as we melted into each other. Albert's hands found my waist as he let his fingers trace my hip bone.

"We should go," he whispered.

"Right," I replied.

He gave me a tiny kiss before pulling me to the elevator. Albert's face held a small smile as he tugged me along. I couldn't help but laugh at the excited expression on his face.

I was expecting to see a restaurant. But no, he drove me to the ocean. It was the same ocean where James had first kissed me, the same beach where I'd started this chaotic journey. And now, I sat staring at the waves with the love of my life.

There was a blanket spread out with two glasses of blood atop it. Beside us was a bowl of cherries, lemons, and limes. Candles were set up in a circle around us. As I sipped from my glass, Albert laid his head against mine. We hadn't talked very much. We'd grown comfortable just holding each other.

"Anne," he whispered.

"Mhm," I replied.

I noticed a small box in his hand. I caught my breath. He smiled softly. Albert knew I understood what was going to happen. Our night had suddenly changed.

"You know what I'm going to ask you," Albert said in a gentle tone.

I smiled. "Yes."

He flipped the box open to reveal a silver ring. There were tiny diamonds embedded in it in the shape of a flower. He took the little diamond rose from the box and slipped it on my finger. I watched it with fascination.

"Ms. Emerson," he whispered. "Will you marry me?"

I traced my finger across his jaw and pressed kisses upon his cheeks. His hands found the pin in my hair and pulled it down. Black curls fell down around my face. He took one strand of hair within his hands and placed a simple kiss upon it. Our eyes locked in a moment of understanding that would last forever.

"Yes," I whispered.

A smile spread across his lips. We just sat there for a few seconds as we were surrounded by our future. His lips brushed mine as he pulled me to his lap. I laced my fingers in his hair as his hands traveled to my thighs. I don't know how long the kiss lasted — it seemed like years. We just sat there watching the waves. For a very long time, I peacefully enjoyed the feel of his hands against my skin. I was going to marry him. Yes, I'd been completely sure of it for a while. But having the ring on my finger signified the change that was occurring. We were finally going to be linked together in every single way I could possibly imagine. I was going to be married to the most amazing, protective, and beautiful man I'd ever met. He was going to be mine for a very long time. Albert and I were a forever love, and I was absolutely thrilled about it.

Coming Soon
Book 3 of the
Shades of Us Trilogy

The Shades of Us Trilogy Book 3

Crimson
Vows

ABBY FARNSWORTH
FROM THE AUTHOR OF THE EVERGREEN TRILOGY

Abby Farnsworth is the YA paranormal and urban fantasy romance author of the EverGreen Trilogy. Her books are targeted toward teens and young adults but can be enjoyed by readers of all ages.

She enjoys traveling, history, and reading a good book. When not working on her next novel, she can be found taking long walks exploring the natural world, trying a new recipe, or singing in various ensembles.

She currently resides in West Virginia with her family but

adores trips to the beach, mountains, cities, and historical landmarks.

To learn more about Abby, her books, and current projects, take a look at the following:
#authorabbyfarnsworth
#theevergreentrilogy
Instagram: @abbyfarnsworth.writer
Facebook: @abbyfarnsworth.writer.poet

www.ingramcontent.com/pod-product-compliance
Lightning Source LLC
Chambersburg PA
CBHW030336180626
46810CB00003B/1375